REMY AND THE ALIEN GIRLS

RILEY ROSE

BOOK TWO IN THE REMY AND THE SEX MONSTERS SERIES

Cover Design by Mahinoor eBooks

Originally published on Kindle Vella as Little Red Riding Slut: Episodes 35-61.

Read all the Episodes of Remy and the Sex Monsters on Kindle Vella

Read Episodes 1-15 in Book 1 - Remy and the Sex Aliens

Sign-Up for my E-Mail List to Stay Up-To-Date on New Releases!

Visit RileyRoseErotica.com for more sexy stories!

Chapter 1

Remy jogged along the wooded path, wearing tiny cotton shorts and a comfy T-shirt adorned with adorable Ewoks. The mountains near her house provided a beautiful landscape and a challenging workout. It was Remy's favorite place to run.

And she was really pushing herself. The non-stop sex with curious aliens, a domineering sex robot, and a horny scientist had amped up her libido, so she figured a punishing run would help expel some of that sexual energy. Not that there was anything wrong with lots of sex. It was great! But she couldn't think of sex 24/7. Well, maybe she could, but she should probably do other things too.

She reached the top of a precipice overlooking a crystal blue lake. This was Remy's favorite spot on the run, and a great place to take a break.

She bent forward, putting her hands on her knees, panting and watching her sweat drip onto the rockface.

Thirty feet below her, the water lapped lazily against the shore. She peered over the edge, deciding if she would finally do it. She had always wanted to try cliff diving, but had chickened out every time. She knew professionals dove off way higher cliffs than this, but looking down, thirty feet seemed like a lot.

But she had so much energy from all the intense fucking, she felt like this was the time to do it. Yeah, she was going to fucking do it!

She took her sneakers off and stripped.

She stood at the edge and closed her eyes, feeling the breeze tickle her nipples and pussy. It felt amazing to be one with nature, listening to the bird calls and the cute critters skittering through the woods. Remy wished she could run around naked more often. Of course, she had barely worn any clothes lately: aliens and sex robots had a poor view of human girls covering up. They were pretty smart that way.

She opened her eyes and jumped.

"Ahhhhhhhh!" she screamed as she plummeted, the wind whipping her hair upward.

She splashed into the lake, dipping below the surface before reemerging like a naked mermaid.

"Woohoo!" she shrieked, slapping the water gleefully. She did it! Her stomach had totally risen into her throat, but it was exhilarating. And the water was pleasantly cool: the perfect tonic to a sweaty run.

She did different strokes around the lake. She was a good swimmer and was always happy when she was in the water. Being naked in the water was even better. Though it might be embarrassing if anyone wandered by. Not many people jogged up here, so she was probably safe. Of course, if someone did mosey up to the lake, it could be kind of hot. Since she left her clothes on top of the precipice, she'd have to exit the water and show the sneaky peeper all her naked assets. Yikes! When did she get so excited about exhibiting her body? Probably when the aliens turned her into their plaything. Ooh, she wondered if the aliens were in their cloaked ship in the sky, watching her skinny dip. Just in case they were, she swam to shallow water and stood, shaking her tits and ass. Any hidden human oglers would hopefully enjoy it too.

She stopped after realizing how silly it was to perform for hidden aliens who probably weren't even there. She better get back to jogging: she was apparently still super-horny.

She waded to the shore, the sunlight glinting off the droplets running down her body. She tossed her long locks behind her and stretched. The sun felt wonderful. It was so nice being naked. Maybe she could start a nudist camp up here, a camp where humans, aliens, and robots were all welcome. And all welcome to have hot sex!

The trees rustled, drawing Remy's attention. "Hey! Are there any sneaky peepers out there?" She put her hands on her hips, then realized that just made it look like she was flaunting her stuff. "Um, and if there are, hope you're enjoying the show!" She blushed immediately, not believing she just blurted that out. She had always had a naughty streak, but was usually too shy to let it out. Fucking aliens and robots had given her a real sexual awakening.

She stepped closer. She couldn't tell if it was a person or an animal. Maybe it was a cute deer that would let her pet it. Okay, that was very unlikely, since deer usually scampered off at the first sight of humans, but she could still hope.

She approached the rustling bushes. From behind them emerged a giant: it was eight feet tall, covered in dark brown fur, and had a shaggy ape-man face.

Remy's jaw dropped as she gazed up at it. Holy shit, it was Bigfoot! Or Sasquatch. Or whatever else you wanted to call it. And it was staring at her naked tits.

She took a step back and tripped over a rock, plopping onto her butt.

The huge creature crashed out of the brush.

Remy scrambled to her feet and ran away like she was in a Scooby-Doo cartoon. "Ahhhhhhh!"

Twigs and branches stung her chest and legs as she barreled through the woods. Sprinting naked in the forest wasn't a great idea, but she certainly wasn't going back for her clothes.

The lumbering beast stomped after her, its footsteps getting closer. Why the heck did Remy keep running into these aliens and cryptids? Couldn't she just be a normal sci-fi-loving girl and dream up stories about them? Of course, that meant she would have missed out on all the intense alien/robot sex. But she didn't know if Bigfoot wanted sex. Maybe it wanted to eat her. Or do whatever Bigfeet liked to do.

She glanced over her shoulder to see how close it was and tripped over a root. She tumbled end over end down a hill, feeling like she was bruising every part of her body.

She crashed into a tree, her head smacking against it.

Her vision faded in and out. The last thing she saw was a huge, furry monster looming over her.

***

Remy woke with a groan. Her head still hurt as did much of the rest of her body.

She stretched gingerly, making sure nothing was broken. Then took in her surroundings.

She was in a cave, light pouring in from the opening about twenty feet away. She was resting on deer pelts laid out like a makeshift bed. They were surprisingly comfortable. As was the cave itself.

A fire crackled in the middle of the ancient abode, casting a pleasant warmth. It was cooler inside the cavern, plus she was naked, so the fire was a welcome sight.

She was about to scoot closer to it when the creature who

had pursued her plodded in with a handcrafted wooden container of berries.

It saw its guest was awake and stared at her.

Remy froze, then realized she was lying in a rather provocative position, resting on her side with her limbs posed like a supermodel.

She sat up, crossed her legs, and waved meekly. "Um, hello, Mr. Bigfoot. D… did you carry me here after I was knocked out?"

The creature grunted and approached her. A tingle of fear shot through Remy, but she suppressed it. If the beast meant her harm, it probably wouldn't have brought her to its home.

It plopped onto the ground and set the container of berries in front of her. It grunted and pointed at the fruit, then at its mouth.

"You want me to eat them?" Remy glanced at the basket: strawberries, raspberries, and blackberries were mixed together, looking nice and juicy. "Okay! I am pretty hungry from jogging, and, um, running away from you."

The creature seemed to frown.

"Oh, I'm sorry, I wasn't saying you're a big meanie or anything. You just surprised me, and I didn't know if you were a nice Bigfoot."

It nodded and pointed at the fruit again.

"Right. I'll just shut up and eat." Remy popped the

berries in her mouth, not wanting to accidentally insult her host. "Mmm, these are delicious!" She gobbled up a bunch more. She was surprised the creature could pick such dainty fruit with his thick fingers. He was apparently quite dexterous. How did she know it was a male? The way he was sitting cross-legged gave her a clear view of the huge appendage between his legs. An appendage that hung limply, which meant it wasn't erect. She could barely fathom how large it would get when the creature got excited.

She felt him staring at her again and turned her gaze from his groin to his eyes. It wasn't polite to gape at someone's penis when you first met.

"Sorry, you just have a huge dick. It's very impressive."

He growled in acknowledgment, seeming to know he had an impressive cock.

He stuck his hand in the basket, sharing the fruit with Remy. Her much smaller fingers brushed his furry ones. It was a soft, pleasant sensation.

"I bet you're a great bed buddy," she told him.

The creature looked at her quizzically.

"Oh," she added hurriedly. "I just meant your fur is so soft, you're probably nice to cuddle with. I didn't mean we should, um, fuck or anything." She glanced at his cock again. Not that she would have said no to having sex with him. That would have seemed preposterous a couple of days ago. But after doing it with aliens and a robot, fucking Sasquatch didn't seem that strange.

He pointed at her breasts, her nipples growing on command. She blushed. Ack! What were her girls doing? A sexy Bigfoot gesturing at them was all it took to get them excited.

"Um, those are my boobs. D… do you like them?"

He nodded rapidly. Oh shit, could he understand her? Or did he just like that she was now pointing at her tits too?

She squeezed her breasts, moving them around. "Yeah, they're pretty cool. And they're, ohhhhhhh, really sensitive." She brushed her nipples as she spoke, making her entire body shiver.

Bigfoot's dick began to grow. He leaned in closer.

"Y… you like that? I can shake them for you if you want."

More vigorous nodding.

She bounced her breasts, putting on the sexiest titty show she could. She was a little embarrassed to be performing for a huge, woodland creature, but it was making her hot, so she kept doing it.

Bigfoot wasn't complaining. He grunted happily as his cock grew larger and larger.

Remy's eyes grew larger and larger as she watched it. Every time she thought his penis was going to stop, it kept growing. She couldn't believe how huge it was. In fact, she couldn't take her eyes off it.

"That's one enormous cock!" she told him unnecessarily. He probably know how big his dick was.

When his little Bigfoot finally stopped growing, it stuck straight out, pointing at Remy's tits and quivering in anticipation.

She gazed at her breasts. Her nipples were inflamed and screaming for attention. And Bigfoot apparently had the cure.

"Y... you want to rub your cock between my tits?"

He growled in affirmation. Well, she assumed it was in affirmation because his dick bobbed more rapidly.

Remy gazed at the monster again. Not Bigfoot but the monster between his legs. If she let him titty fuck her, that would probably lead to her sucking his cock. And that would probably lead to him shoving his hugeness in her tight pussy. And eventually up her even tighter ass.

But he was bigger than the aliens and even the hugest attachment T-69 possessed. Was she ready to go full beast mode?

Hell yeah!

She got onto her knees and held her breasts apart for him.

It was time for a Bigfoot boob fucking!

Chapter 2

Remy pressed her breasts against her beastly lover's huge cock. "Holy crap, you're so big!" She had already told him that, but she figured like most human males, he probably enjoyed having his man, er, Bigfoot-hood complimented.

He grunted and put two hairy paws on her shoulders, thrusting between her breasts.

"Oh wow!" Remy loved how his monstrosity massaged her tits. And he loved it too, based on the pleasurable moans he made. Remy smiled, knowing she could add cryptids to the list of creatures who enjoyed her boobs.

Of course, her tits weren't the only thing getting massaged. He was so huge his cock rubbed up and down her face. So she did the only natural thing: she stuck her tongue out and licked every thrust of his penis.

He really liked that. He titty fucked her harder, whacking her face and making her feel like his submissive whore.

She played with her nipples, cooing contentedly as his dick rubbed across her lips. She wondered if she'd be able to fit him in her mouth. She had a feeling she would soon find out.

He groaned more loudly, his large eyes rolling into the back of his furry head.

"Um, are you going to cum?" Remy asked. He was certainly making similar noises to human boys before they ejaculated. Though his were more feral and enticing.

Bigfoot answered by shooting his seed all over her face. He roared in pleasure as his cock erupted like a volcano. He drenched her face and hair and then pulled back to spray it all over her tits.

Remy's jaw dropped. She had never seen so much cum shoot out of a penis before. Of course, with her mouth open, she got plenty of his seed down her throat. He tasted like the forest, fresh and earthy. It wasn't bad. She wouldn't have any problem guzzling him down if he wanted to deep throat her. Oh boy, she was really becoming slutty if her first thought after getting a Bigfoot cum bath was to suck his huge dick. But it wasn't her fault. How could a girl not be slutty when all these aliens, robots, and cryptids couldn't keep their cocks out of her naughty holes?

He shot a few more loads across her body, then sat back and sighed. Remy had another satisfied customer.

She examined her body: it was dripping with Sasquatch seed from head to toe. "Boy, you can really cum. I'm drenched!"

He snatched her with one hand, tossed her over his

shoulder, and stomped out of the cave.

"Where are we going?" Remy asked as her butt bounced besides his massive head. She was impressed by how strong he was. He lifted her like she was weightless. She daydreamed about what he could do to her with those powerful Bigfoot arms.

He grunted something in return, but Remy hadn't mastered Sasquatch speech. "I wasn't complaining about being covered in cum," she told him, worried she might have insulted him. She didn't know the intricacies of cryptid cultural norms. "You can cum on me whenever you want." She had learned to be very open to receiving her lovers' sticky gifts the past two days.

He didn't reply, marching them in silence until they reached the lake where they first met.

Remy wondered if he brought her here because of how picturesque it was. Maybe he was taking her on a romantic date. That was sweet! She had never dated a mythical monster before.

But instead of spreading out a blanket for a picnic, he hurled her into the water.

"Ahhhhh!" She flew twenty feet in the air before splashing into the lake.

She resurfaced, sputtering water out of her nose. "What the heck was that?"

Bigfoot waded into the wetness. He was so tall he could

stand even in the deeper parts of the lake.

He splashed water over himself and then pointed at Remy.

"Ohhh," she said as she treaded water. "You brought me here so I can clean off your yummy cum. Thanks!"

He nodded and raised her out of the water. He grabbed her ankle, inverted her, and repeatedly plunged her headfirst in and out of the depths.

"Ack!" she yelled as she broke the surface. "Is this the way you wash your mates?" Back down she went. Apparently so. Well, it was a little unorthodox, but who was she to argue with Bigfoot bathing rituals?

After several dunkings, he lifted her out of the water. She hung upside down, droplets running down, or rather up, her nude body. She was eye-level with his crotch. Which meant she had a wonderful view of his once-again erect penis.

"Wow, you have an impressive recovery period. I bet all the Sasquatch ladies love you." She glanced up at him. "Um, are there any Sasquatch ladies?" Remy realized her new friend might be alone in the world, with none of his species remaining. That was sad. But Remy was determined to cheer him up.

"While I'm down here, would you like me to suck your huge cock?" It was throbbing before her, almost bumping against her nose. It obviously needed nice human lips around it.

Remy leaned forward and kissed the tip of his penis. It twitched and pressed forward, indicating she should open her mouth for it.

She did and licked his bulbous head. Bigfoot moaned. His body shook. And then his cock was in her mouth.

Remy's gasp was muffled by the sheer size of him. Only his head was inside her, but even that was making her mouth feel stuffed.

She sucked him off like a dutiful Sasquatch slut. And she was happy to see him return the favor.

He spread her legs and brought his mouth to her pussy. His long tongue lashed out, licking up and down her slit.

Remy trembled and moaned into his cock. Fuck, that was one amazing tongue. It was much larger than a human's and coarser, which allowed it to stimulate her lips much better.

She took more of him in her mouth, wanting to prove she could satisfy him. At the same time, his tongue penetrated her tight barrier. It was so powerful, it was like a cock piercing her lips. Her shrieks were dampened by his huge beasthood, but they were enough to tell him to forage deeper into her wetness.

They both continued their exploration of their lover's most sensitive parts. Remy took more of his cock down her throat. Bigfoot wormed deeper into her pussy.

He wrapped his arms around her waist, pressing her to

him tightly as they pleasured each other. She never thought she'd be doing a standing sixty-nine with Sasquatch. But she loved new sexual experiences. The past two days had provided a lifetime's worth of those. And she knew Bigfoot was going to provide a bunch more.

His tongue was so deep in her, filling her in a rough, animalistic way. She didn't mind. It felt great and spurred her to suck his cock even harder. She couldn't believe how much of him she had gotten in her mouth. It wasn't all of his enormous shaft. That would have been impossible. But it was at least a good two-thirds. Remy was proud of her deep-throating prowess. The aliens and T-69 had provided great training in being a big slut!

Bigfoot's cock trembled and expanded. She knew he was about to burst. So was she. He had been tongue-lashing her pussy like it was the cozy cavern he slept in and had her on the verge of an epic orgasm.

They came together. He shot his impressive load into her mouth. It was so forceful she had no choice but to swallow it. She fought to gulp it down without choking. It was difficult with how much cum he was releasing, but she did her best.

He had an easier time lapping up her juices. His larger mouth was well-suited to receive her squirting nectar. In fact, he seemed to find it very tasty: he licked her pussy lips eagerly, trying to get every ounce of girl juice off her.

That made Remy want to guzzle his gift even more. She loved guys who were eager to eat her out. This Sasquatch knew how to please a lady. Which meant Remy was totally going to let him use his ridiculously huge cock to fuck her in any hole he wanted.

She gasped when he finally removed his penis, cum dripping off her lips. He dunked her a few more times to clean off the fresh stickiness, then turned her right-side up.

He held her tightly as she helped clean him. "You really know your way around a pussy," she told him.

He grunted and nodded, like that was an obvious statement. Maybe Sasquatches were renowned for their cunnilingus abilities. What a great species!

He took her in his arms and waded out of the water. She felt like his Bigfoot bride, being carried on their honeymoon. She wondered where his species liked to go on romantic vacations? Somewhere similar to his natural forest? Or would he like to get away to a sunny Caribbean beach? She giggled, picturing him in Bermuda shorts and lounging on a beach chair. His fur would probably be great protection against any nasty burns.

The sun shone brightly above them, which meant it wouldn't take too long to dry. Remy gazed up at her wet, fuzzy lover. "Do you want to lay out by the lake while we dry off?"

He had a different idea on how to spend the time. He

grabbed her hips and held her in front of him, right over his very erect cock.

"Oh! Well, having sex will generate a lot of heat, so that's a good way to dry off too. You're pretty smart!"

He nodded, appreciating her acknowledgment of Bigfoot braininess.

Remy fidgeted as he lowered her towards his quivering beast. Somehow it looked even more monstrous now that it was about to enter her pussy. "C... can you just put the tip in first, Mr. Bigfoot? I don't think I can take you all at once. You're one huge beast!"

He emitted what sounded like a chuckle. Apparently, he knew he had to be delicate with human girls and their tiny pussies. Wait, how many girls had he fucked? Did he prowl the woods looking for nubile nymphs to take back to his cave and give them the most amazing sex of their lives? That was an excellent way to spend time in the woods.

The head of his penis touched her lips. She gasped and clutched his wet fur. Holy crap, she was really going to do it: she was going to let this gigantic creature penetrate her and own her womanhood.

She closed her eyes, trying to prepare herself for his initial thrust.

Nothing could have prepared her for that though. He pushed upward, spreading her lips to their full width and gaining entry to her inner sanctum.

A voiceless cry escaped her lips as she looked to the heavens. She had never felt anything like it, never felt like her pussy was so fully under the power of a penis, never felt like her vagina had been waiting its entire life for a cryptid cock.

She buried her face in his chest and prepared herself for the deepest, most savage fucking of her life.

She loved being a Sasquatch slut!

Chapter 3

"Ohhhh fuucckkk! You destroyed my pussy!"

Bigfoot gazed down at Remy, curious at her outburst.

She blushed. Only the tip of his cock was inside her, and she was already acting like he had fucked her a hundred times in a row.

"Sorry, Mr. Furry, you really didn't destroy my pussy," she explained. "I'm just practicing for when you get fully inside me. I figure if I get a bunch of slutty screams out in advance, it will make it easier to take you."

That got her an even more curious look.

She bit her lip. "Okay, maybe it doesn't make sense. But I'm a weird girl. You'll get used to me."

The only thing the huge creature wanted to get used to at the moment was her pussy. He inched her down his massive cock, which throbbed powerfully, eager to get a taste of a human vagina.

She dug her fingers into his fur and moaned into his chest. God, it was so big. It was barely inside her, and she already felt like she was going to burst. If she managed to take his whole cock, she knew she'd become a Sasquatch slut for eternity. She wouldn't be able to resist taking him whenever he commanded her to strip and get on all fours. She figured he'd want to do it doggy, or Bigfoot, style at some point.

He lowered her another inch. Every movement was agony, but in the best possible way. Her pussy was screaming at her for allowing such a behemoth inside, but also begging for more, pleading to be dominated by the monster cock worming inside it.

In these situations, Remy always went with the slutty side of her pussy. She could take a little pain if it meant she'd get plowed by a strong and sexy Sasquatch. Was he sexy? Remy didn't know what constituted a handsome Bigfoot, but he was cute in a super-hairy way. Thanks to her alien and robot fuckings, she had learned to be very open when it came to new lovers. While a lot of people might think it was strange to fuck Bigfoot, Remy thought it was perfectly natural. He had needs too, right? It was Remy's duty to provide sexual pleasure for him. Wait, that made her sound like his courtesan or sexy servant? Ooh, what if she became a courtesan for every supernatural creature on the planet and every alien around the galaxy? She could travel the globe and to distant worlds, pleasuring the strangest and largest creatures she could find!

Remy shook herself out of her daydream. Oh boy, she was becoming more of a horny slut every day. It was all those aliens' fault. And Sam's thanks to her crazy sex robot. And this huge Bigfoot's. Or maybe Remy was just a closet nympho and had been craving cryptid cock her whole life. She was okay with that. If she was a nympho, at least she was a sexy, sci-fi loving one.

More of his little Bigfoot filled her. Her brain was barely functioning. Her body had been taken over by her pussy, which throbbed, burned, and strained to contain the monster within it.

He reached her cervix, and she shook all over. "Ohhhhhhhhhh Godddddddddd! I've never been so full!!"

Her furry lover grunted in approval of her slutty moans. His hairy hands slid to her ass, enveloping her tan cheeks.

Tremors shot up and down her body. She clung to Bigfoot, trying to adjust to his ridiculous girth. He gave her time to adapt, squeezing her butt.

"Ohhhhhh," she moaned. "Y… you like my booty?"

He roared in response. She took that as an enthusiastic affirmative.

"C… cool. I like creatures who enjoy my butt!"

He enjoyed it a bunch more, feeling it up like he owned it. He definitely owned her pussy. It was impossible for her to be any fuller than she was. She didn't even know how she was fitting him inside. But she was, and she loved it!

Her nipples became hardened points, rubbing against his fur. Her entire body felt like it was one huge erogenous zone.

"P… please fuck me, Mr. Bigfoot," Remy pleaded.

He raised her slowly up his shaft. She moaned along every inch. And moaned even louder as he slid her back down.

"Oh my God, I'll be your forest whore forever!"

He took that as a signal to fuck her harder. He moved her up and down on his cock, easily manipulating her tinier body.

Her legs slipped off his hips, dangling in the air as he rammed her harder.

"Ohhhhhhh… such… a… big… cock!" she got out between moans. It smashed into her harder and faster. It engorged her, touched every part of her, and made her feel completely subservient to him.

"Fuck, fuck, fuck, fuck, fuuuuuccckkkk! You're going to make me your personal slut if you keep pounding my pussy like that!"

He obviously liked the idea of having a personal girl slut, so he pounded her even harder, her ass jiggling like it was in a sexual hurricane.

His body tensed, and his roars increased. Remy gasped: oh fuck, he was about to cum. She had never had Sasquatch seed in her before. Of course, until a few days ago, she had never had alien or robot cum in her either. It was good to experience lots of different flavors of semen. That way she could decide which was her favorite. Oh crap, that's what a super-slut would say, huh? Um, well, sign her up for being a super-slut!

Bigfoot tilted his head back and let out the hugest roar Remy had ever heard: louder than any bear, wolf, or mountain lion. And his climax was just as powerful as his screams. A thick stream exploded up into her. She wailed and squirmed, feeling like it was about to launch her off his cock. She had never experienced such an intense blast of semen before.

"Oh fuck!" she squealed. "You're overloading my pussy!"

He bombarded her with a few more spurts, then pulled out, spewing the rest of his seed across her back and buttocks. It was much stickier than human cum and felt like it belonged on her ass.

He rubbed his erupting penis along her slit and clit and had her joining his climax in no time.

She screamed and squirted, limbs flailing in the air as her juices splattered the forest floor. His cum poured out of her overloaded hole, joining the puddle she was making.

He plopped onto the ground and rested against a tree, cradling her in his massive arms.

She snuggled into him, smearing his fur with the rest of her cum and feeling his stickiness all over her. "Mmm, you're nice and warm." She rubbed his chest, content to cuddle with him for as long as he wanted.

He stroked her hair, examining strands as they sifted through his fingers.

"Oh, yeah, you don't have hair like me, huh? Some of us humans like to grow our hair long. That way we can whip it around all sexy-like to attract a hunky Bigfoot. And you can pull it to make me feel like a submissive slut!"

He tugged on her hair, not enough to hurt, but enough to turn her on.

"Yeah, just like that! You're a quick learner. Or did you already know how to turn girls into sluts?"

He made that chuckling noise again.

She wrinkled her nose. "Hey, exactly how many women have you fucked up here?"

He scratched his head, seeming to not understand her query.

"Okay, then I'll assume I'm your first human conquest. That way I'll go down in the record books. Um, though I'm not sure if there are any record books for that sort of thing. If there are, I bet I just set the record for fucking aliens, a robot, and a Sasquatch in one week."

He scratched his head some more.

"Oh, sorry. Basically, what I'm saying is, I've been a huge monster slut the past few days."

He nodded and wrapped his cozy arms around her.

She giggled. "Glad you approve of me being a monster

slut." She closed her eyes and enjoyed the warmth on her skin, both from the sun and his body.

They took a quick nap together. He was very easy to fall asleep on: he was the furriest and most comfortable lover she had ever been with.

She stretched when she awoke, her pussy feeling sore but satisfied. Very satisfied. Bigfoot knew how to treat a girl's cooch right!

She stared up at his ape-man face. He was kinda cute, as ape-men went.

She knelt on his lap and put her hands on his cheeks. His face cheeks, not his butt cheeks. Not that she would have minded grabbing those. He had felt up her ass a whole bunch, so it was only fair that she get to examine his hairy tush.

"Is it okay if I kiss you?" she asked.

She got a quizzical grunt in reply. It was hard to communicate since she didn't speak the language of the Bigfeet.

But she figured she'd give smooching him a try and see if he liked it. She pressed her lips against his much larger ones. His were coarser than a human's but they moistened at her touch. He didn't seem to understand what she was doing, but as she continued to kiss him gently, he moved his lips in time with hers.

She took his arms and tugged them, indicating he should

wrap them around her. He did and she placed her hands against his chest.

She taught him how to smooch, increasing the intensity as he got the hang of it. It was a little weird but mostly nice. She felt safe and cozy in his arms. She didn't want to leave his embrace. She'd be content to kiss and made love to him in the forest for the rest of the week. Heck, maybe the whole summer.

He got so good at kissing she felt he was ready to graduate to tongue action. She slipped her tongue inside his mouth and showed him how to French kiss. His tongue was so big, he dominated her mouth: it was the most intense tongue-on-tongue action Remy had experienced. There were a lot of nice things about romancing a Bigfoot.

He smiled at her when their lips finally parted. She rubbed her cheek against his. She should totally teach a cryptid romance course. She could help creatures and humans come together to have hot monster sex!

He took her back to his cave where he fucked her on all fours, fucked her cowgirl style, and fucked her in virtually every position found in the Kama Sutra. She wondered if he had managed to get a copy of that book and had studied it intensely. She definitely approved of his taste in literature.

She spent the night in his arms, snuggling on the deer skins in his warm abode. She didn't want to make her way back through the forest in the dark: she wasn't even sure she could walk after how many times he had rammed her with his huge cock. Plus, he was cozier than her favorite blanket. She dozed off as soon he wrapped his arms around her and slept soundly until the chirping birds woke her in the morning.

He brought her more berries for breakfast plus a fried something or other. She didn't recognize what kind of animal it was, but she was starving and didn't want to refuse his hospitality. She bit into the charred meat. It wasn't half bad. She ate it eagerly along with the berries, getting food over her face. Bigfoot didn't keep napkins in his cave.

She would have been happy to spend another day enjoying his company and his cock, but she had to get ready for a date with Sam. The kooky scientist had promised to treat her to dinner for testing out her sex robot.

Remy knew Bigfoot couldn't really understand her. So she grabbed a stick and drew diagrams in the dirt, showing a stick-figure version of her going back to her house. Then she drew herself returning to Bigfoot's cave to show she planned to spend more sex-filled nights with him.

He nodded and escorted her back to the path, lifting her up by her rump to give her a kiss.

He set her back down and, with a slap on the ass, set her on her way.

She retrieved her clothes and phone, glad they were still where she had left them. She hopped into her shorts and shirt and was halfway down the mountain when a familiar blue-white light surrounded her from above.

She was transported in an instant onto an alien ship. And not just any alien ship: the same one she had been fucked on repeatedly just a few days ago.

The five big-dicked aliens stood before her, cocks at the ready.

But this time, they had a friend with them.

Remy gasped. A new sexy alien to fuck!

She was one lucky girl!

Chapter 4

Remy's gaze flicked from the five alien cocks to the alien pussy next to them. Oh crap, her gray alien buddies had an alien girl with them.

She was humanoid, but her skin was blue and she had thick tendrils instead of hair. Ooh, just like a Twi'lek. Everyone knew they were the sexiest Star Wars girls. This woman had more hair tendrils than a Twi'lek, four instead of two, but had the same lovely tits, hips, and legs as the sci-fi hotties. And while she couldn't see it at the moment, Remy bet the alien had a super-hot ass.

Remy hopped up and down, unintentionally making her boobs bounce. "Oh my God, a real-life sexy, blue alien girl! I'm so happy!"

"Why thank you," the alien replied in perfect English. "It's lovely to meet you too."

Remy gasped. "You can speak my language?"

She nodded, her tendrils swaying in a hypnotic way. "I have the ability to instantly learn any language upon hearing it. It's quite handy in inter-galactic travel."

Remy did more hopping, and, thus, more boob bouncing.

"That's the coolest power ever! It's so nice to be able to talk to an alien."

The woman motioned to the five gray aliens. "Yes, they unfortunately don't possess the same ability, but they've been communicating with me telepathically."

Remy stopped bouncing. "What?! That's amazing! Why can't I talk to them that way?"

The blue girl tilted her head to the side, listening to an unspoken conversation. "They say your species doesn't have to ability to make a telepathic link with them."

Remy pouted. "Boo! That sucks."

The woman sashayed over to Remy, moving her hips in ways only alien girls could. She looked a little older than Remy in human years, but Remy didn't know if her species aged the same way.

She put a gentle hand on Remy's shoulder. "Don't worry, my lovely human. I'll translate anything they want to communicate to you."

"Oh, that's so nice of you!" Remy shivered from the woman's close proximity. Her nude body was very enticing, and her face was prettier than virtually any human girl Remy had ever seen. "Um, did they abduct you to conduct sexy experiments too?"

The alien girl smiled. "Yes. I was quite surprised when they took me from my planet. But when they explained they were merely curious how different species expressed sexuality, I was more than happy to help. Their dicks are quite delicious."

"Tell me about it!" Remy replied. "They fucked me so hard and made me pleasure them all at once."

The woman's smile broadened. "Yes, they say you admitted to being a human slut quite often."

Remy blushed. "Ahh! They didn't have to tell you that."

"Oh, don't worry. They told me every single naughty thing they did to you. And even showed me the holo-recordings."

Remy's face turned redder than a sunburn. "Ack! I'm so embarrassed." She knew those recordings would come back to haunt her. Though part of her was turned on that this sexy, blue alien chick had watched her become the gray aliens' sex toy.

The alien woman rubbed Remy's back. "Don't be embarrassed. It was the sexiest thing I've ever seen. I can see why they're so infatuated with humanity."

Remy's blush turned into a smile. This alien lady was so sweet. "Oh, th… thank you."

"What's your name, beautiful human girl?"

Remy tingled. She really liked this alien hottie complimenting her. "Remy."

"Remy," the woman repeated, testing out the name. "We don't have names like that among my species, but it's quite lovely."

More tingling. This girl was really good at flirting. Remy was totally falling for her. "Aw, thanks! What's your name?"

"Kigami-Rahntamini-Zunfiani."

"Wow. You have a long name."

"That's just my proper name. My full name is much longer and comprises family, clan, and province names."

Remy's eyes widened. Yikes! She had so much to learn about alien cultures. And she wanted to learn everything she could. And if that learning happened through hot, submissive sex, she'd just have to surrender her body to these horny aliens. "Um, can I just call you Kigami?"

"You may."

"Great. It's a pleasure to meet you!" Remy thrust her hand out.

Kigami stared at it.

"Oh, it's a human greeting ritual," Remy explained. "You take my hand and we shake up and down."

"Ah, I see." She took Remy's hand and did an awkward shake. "It's good to learn alien customs."

Remy smiled. That's right. She was the alien from their viewpoint, and her human customs were probably quite strange to them. "I agree. I want to learn all about your species and the horny gray aliens too."

Kigami smiled. "I'd be happy to teach you. But first, our curious captors believe you are wearing too much."

Remy glanced down at her shorts and T-shirt. "Oh, I can

strip."

"There's no need." Kigami stepped back, and one of the gray aliens pointed a ray gun at Remy.

She held up her hands. "No, wait..."

He shot her with a white beam, disintegrating all her clothing.

"Hey! Why do you aliens have to keep destroying all my clothes?"

"Oh, is clothing important to humans?" Kigami asked.

"Um, well, sort of. We don't run around naked all the time."

Kigami raised her eyebrows. "Really? How odd. We're always naked on my planet."

Now Remy was the one raising her eyebrows. "I need to visit your planet immediately!"

The blue goddess laughed. It was deeper than most human girls' laughs, but very pleasant and alluring. "Perhaps I will get to take you there one day."

Remy jumped up and down again, this time really making her boobs bounce since there was nothing containing them. She had always dreamed about visiting faraway planets and hanging out with cool and sexy aliens. "That would be amazing!"

"But you'd have to be naked."

"I can do that! I've spent a lot of time in the buff recently."

"Good. Because these aliens require you to always be naked on their ship. As you can see, they do not wear clothing."

Remy surveyed the small gray bodies with the large gray dicks. It was true: the aliens had been fully nude the last time she was on their ship. "Okay! It's their ship so it's only right to follow their rules."

Kigami glanced at the male aliens, communicating their response. "They believe you are an accommodating human and believe they chose correctly in making you their first human slut."

Remy did more excited hopping. "Really? I was their first human girl? What an honor!" She stopped hopping. "Wait, did they choose me because they thought I was the biggest slut on the planet?" Remy had sure been acting slutty lately, but she wasn't sure she deserved that moniker.

"No. They had never seen a female with curves like yours and wanted to explore your nude body."

Remy blushed. "Oh my God, that's so flattering! They really explored it last time. Like every inch of it."

Kigami nodded. "I know what you mean. They probed every hole they could find on me."

"Wasn't it great?" Remy tingled, thinking back to the decadent devices the aliens shoved in her.

"It was quite intoxicating. But they wish us to do something else this time."

Remy's interest was piqued. "Even bigger probes?"

"No. They wish to watch us make love."

Remy's job dropped. She was going to get to have sex with this ridiculously hot, blue alien girl? Hell yeah! "I would love to fuck you!"

"Oh, good. I have been eager to explore your human body ever since they showed me all the videos of you."

Remy went back to blushing. "Ahh! How many videos of me do they have?"

"Quite a few. I especially enjoyed the one from yesterday of you fucking that huge, hairy creature."

Remy didn't think her face could get any redder than it currently was. "You guys were watching me fuck Bigfoot?"

"Is that the creature's name? It certainly does have big feet. But you seemed to be most interested in its big cock."

Remy covered her face. She was so mortified. She had no idea the aliens had been peeping on her earthly sexual activities. Those little sneaks.

She peeked between her fingers. "Um, they didn't save that recording of me and Bigfoot did they?"

"Of course they did. They seem to be fascinated watching you have sex. And I can't say I blame them."

Remy hid behind her hands again but peeked out one more time when she heard a familiar noise: her sexual moans. A holo-screen floated above her, showing her and Bigfoot by the lake, her furry lover raising her up and down on his massive cock.

"Oh my God, that's me!"

"Yes," Kigami replied. "The creature is fucking you very vigorously."

Remy watched Bigfoot slam her rapidly on his Sasquatch salami. She wanted to run and hide, but she couldn't take her eyes off the holo. Watching Bigfoot dominate her was almost as exciting as Bigfoot actually dominating her.

Kigami and the aliens were glued to the screen, only flicking it off once Bigfoot had unloaded his cum inside Remy.

"They've been watching that almost non-stop," the lovely blue girl told her.

"Oh no!" Remy wailed. "I've become an alien porn star!"

Kigami rubbed Remy's shoulder. "Don't worry. They're only keeping it for their own research."

Remy laughed. "Research? Geez, alien guys use the same excuse as human guys. They just want to jerk off watching me get fucked."

Kigami nodded. "Yes. They've spilled much of their seed watching that particular holo."

Remy blushed again. "I'm really not that much of a slut."

"The video evidence would indicate otherwise."

"Ahh! Okay, I'm a slut. But I only became one recently. After my first encounter with these aliens actually."

Kigami moved closer and rubbed both of Remy's arms.

"Don't worry. I love to fuck too. People who have lots of sex are highly regarded among my people."

Remy clasped her hands together. "Your people sound amazing!" Now she really needed to visit Kigami's planet.

"I like it. I cum a lot!"

Remy bounced up and down. "You're such a cool girl! I feel like we're going to become best friends."

"If you keep shaking your breasts like that, we definitely will."

Both of them giggled and shook their tits.

The gray aliens's cocks expanded and bobbed up and down, excited by the nude females frolicking.

"So, um, how do they want us to fuck?" Remy asked her new alien friend. "Fingering? Eating each other out?"

"Nope. They want me to fuck you with my tendrils." The four tentacles on her head expanded, growing down her back until they reached her knees.

Remy's eyes widened. The tentacles were long and huge and were apparently going in her pussy.

God, she loved aliens!

Chapter 5

Kigami's tendrils snaked along Remy's naked flesh. "Have you ever been with a girl with appendages like this?"

"N… no," Remy replied, squirming under the alien woman's tantalizing tentacle touch.

"Do you like how they feel?" The tendrils roamed across Remy's hips and thighs, massaging her gently.

"Ohhhh yes." Remy closed her eyes, melting into the alien girl's tender caresses.

Kigami pulled Remy against her, their breasts touching, their lips inches apart. Her hair tentacles wormed along Remy's ass, squeezing and playing with it.

"Oh God, that feels good," Remy purred. She never knew she would have such a thing for tentacles. Maybe it was all those hours watching *hentai* videos.

Kigami ran her fingers through Remy's hair. "I've never seen such strange sprouts emanating from a skull."

"Hey!" Remy pouted. "Most people think I have sexy hair." Her brunette locks spilled well past her shoulders, perfect for being yanked while getting frisky.

"My apologies. I did not mean your hair isn't fetching. I

just have not seen such a thing before. Your strands are very soft and silky."

Remy smiled. "That's much better. That's how you get a human girl to spread her legs for you."

"Or I could do this." Kigami ran one of her tendrils between Remy's thighs, parting them, before rubbing along her slit.

"Ohhhhhh, th… that works too," Remy moaned. The tentacle secreted some kind of fluid that helped it easily slide along Remy's lips. She clasped Kigami's shoulders, eager for more.

Two tendrils were busy with her butt, one was obsessed with her slit, and the fourth sneaked between her breasts, titty fucking her.

"Ohhhh! You really put your tendrils to good use."

"Yes. It leaves my hands free to play with your hair. I'm fascinated by it." She sifted through Remy's long locks, seemingly wanting to touch every strand.

Remy loved it. Kigami had such a gentle touch, with both her fingers and her tentacles.

She glanced over her lover's shoulder. The five male aliens stroked their cocks, staring at the girls with unblinking eyes.

"I think they like what we're doing," Remy said.

"I think they'll like this even more." The blue bombshell slid her titty-fucking tendril up to Remy's lips.

"You want me to suck you off?"

"Yes. I need your human lips around me."

"Okay!" Remy was eager to see what a female alien tendril tasted like. She bet it'd be yummy!

Kigami slipped between Remy's lips. The sci-fi loving girl tasted the alien's secretion: it wasn't exactly like anything found on Earth, but it was kind of close to an apricot-honey mix. So she was right: super-yummy!

Just as Remy was fitting more of Kigami in her mouth, the sexy alien penetrated Remy's lower lips.

"Mrmph!!" she gasped into the tentacle filling her throat. Kigami had given her a surprise pussy fucking. Which were totally the best kind.

"Ohhhhh," the blue creature moaned. "Are all Earth girls this tight?"

Remy tried to reply that she hadn't sampled the entire female population of the planet, so she wasn't really sure. But it just came out as sexy gobbledygook. One thing was sure: Kigami thought Remy had an amazing pussy. So Remy had to represent her fellow human girls and their tight cooches. She could do it!

Kigami snatched Remy's hips. "I must get as deep as possible in you. Your pussy's intoxicating!"

Remy squealed into the tendril in her mouth. She loved fucking aliens who were drunk on her pussy. And, boy, did Kigami ever get deep. Her tentacle wormed all the way inside. It was thicker than most human cocks, but its slimy secretions helped it easily slide in and out of Remy's tight folds.

"Let's give our voyeurs a better view." Kigami spun Remy around so she faced the aliens, her butt bumping against Kigami's bare, blue pussy. One tentacle was still in Remy's mouth and another in her pussy. Kigami used the other two to snatch Remy's arms and tie them behind her back.

Remy wiggled under her alien mistress's touch: being bound by tentacles was hot!

Kigami continued to titty fuck Remy, the same tendril getting deeper in her throat. Remy loved giving sexy, intergalactic blowjobs.

The gray aliens moved closer, stroking their huge cocks vigorously.

Kigami reached around and took two big handfuls of Remy's tits. She played with the human slut's nipples, easily getting them to poke out. Remy always had a problem with them showing underneath her T-shirts. Hey, could she help it that she had horny, pokey nips?

The super-hot alien rammed Remy harder while rubbing her pussy against Remy's juicy ass. Remy felt alien juices coat her cheeks. She wondered if Kigami's pussy tasted as good as her tentacles. She had a feeling she was going to find out.

Kigami pounded Remy's pussy and throat until her tentacles seized up and expelled tasty blue liquid into both holes.

Remy squealed, unprepared for the tentacles to expel alien girl cum. It was blue and milky: just like the bantha milk found in her favorite galaxy far, far away. There was no way Remy was going to pass up drinking the same milk as Luke Skywalker. Though she was more like Remy Slutwalker right now. She gulped down Kigami's yummy juice as her pussy greedily sucked in similar juice down below.

Remy trembled as round after round of alien cum was pumped into her. And onto her: the five gray aliens got so excited they all ejaculated at once, their creamy jizz splattering Remy from head to toe.

Kigami finally pulled out, dribbling blue sauce along Remy's lips and tits. The same aqua liquid poured out of Remy's pussy, her cunt having been overloaded with Kigami's gift.

Remy shivered in her lover's arms, staring at the different flavors of extraterrestrial cum adorning her body. And that's when it became official: she was going to be an alien slut forever.

"You are very sticky," Kigami commented.

"Yup. I spend a lot of time covered in cum." Well, at least lately she did. She had been on a non-stop alien/sex robot/Bigfoot fuck-a-thon.

"You are a wise human."

Remy giggled. She liked alien cultures who thought being covered in cum was a sign of intelligence.

Kigami glanced at the other aliens. "They tell me you especially enjoy being probed up your tight ass."

"God, I love it!" Remy shouted. Then blushed. She hadn't intended to be that exuberant about it. "I mean, I recently became an anal slut, and I can't seem to get enough of it."

"It's fortunate that I'm here, then. I love probing tight asses." And with that she shoved one of her tendrils up Remy's butt.

"Holy alien ass fuckings!!" Remy's body tensed and her ass clenched the juicy tentacle. Kigami was a master at surprise penetration.

"On your knees, please," Kigami said. Remy complied. She could never turn down a polite request like that.

The alien girl shoved another tendril in Remy's pussy. She was using the two tendrils that had previously bound Remy's arms, giving the two that had ejaculated a chance to recuperate.

"You're going to ride my tendrils while our alien captors take turns fucking your mouth."

Remy shivered. "Oh my God, you guys are making me the biggest alien slut ever!"

"Yes. It's quite fun, isn't it?"

"So much fun!" Remy agreed.

"Great. Now start fucking my tendrils."

Remy moved her hips up and down, making love to Kigami's juicy appendages. Her ass strained to take the tentacle, but that just made Remy want it more.

The alien girl knelt behind her, guiding Remy's hips as her other two tendrils massaged the human slut's tits.

Remy sighed. It was so nice to be with a lover that had so many ways to play with her body.

The gray aliens were ready to play with her mouth. One of them stepped forward and pressed his cock against her lips.

Remy opened her mouth and took him. She had gotten a lot of practice sucking these aliens off during their first encounter, so she knew what they liked.

She deep throated him, sucking him hard so he would have no choice but to jizz into her mouth.

Kigami encouraged her to fuck her tentacles faster. Remy slammed her hips up and down, taking more and more of the blue tendrils.

"You are very eager to have all three of your holes fucked," Kigami remarked.

"Mmm hrmph!" Remy gagged into the alien cock. She was very eager. Nothing made her feel sluttier than being fucked in the mouth, pussy, and ass all at once.

Kigami took an appendage off Remy's right breast and

slipped it underneath her until it reached her clit. The sexy alien rubbed up and down it, adding a fourth flavor to the intense fucking Remy was receiving.

Remy's hips spasmed. Damn, tentacles were perfect for manipulating sensitive clits. And Remy's was crazy sensitive. It burst out of its hood, burning with desire. Her clit was a horny little sucker!

"The alien is about to cum," Kigami helpfully informed Remy. "He would like you to gulp down everything he offers while you fuck my tendrils as hard as you can."

Remy uttered another incomprehensible affirmation. It was hard to talk with a big alien dick in your mouth.

She slammed herself as fast as she could on the dual tentacles, her pussy and ass blazing like an inferno.

The alien matched her speed, ramming his throbbing cock between her lips. He tightened and then exploded, shooting his milky cum from his non-existent balls. Remy still hadn't figured out where they kept their juicy jizz. But they could sure produce a lot of it.

While Remy was guzzling alien cum, Kigami yanked her human friend's clit and made her experience her own spillage. The sticky slut squirted onto the smooth, metallic floor of the alien ship.

Kigami wanted in on the fun too, so she let her tendrils release their thick liquid into Remy's pussy and ass.

"Mmmmmmrrrppphhhh!" the beautiful co-ed moaned,

realizing she was getting alien cum in all three holes. Fuck, it was so amazing. And, fuck, she felt so slutty. She wanted Kigami and the gray aliens to dominate her across the galaxy.

The alien male pulled out and shot the last bit of his load across her face.

"Ack!" Remy yelped. "Alien guys are just like human guys. They love cumming on girls' faces."

Kigami patted Remy's shoulders. "I think that's common to all male species."

Remy nodded. She appreciated that sex was universal.

"Do you mind if they splatter your lovely face?" her blue friend asked.

"Not at all. Everyone's been cumming all over my face the past couple of days."

Kigami pinched Remy's tush. "The grays were right. You are an accommodating human."

"I aim to please! Especially when sexy aliens are involved."

"Great. Because you have four more cocks to pleasure."

Remy's eyes widened as the next big alien dick approached. Damn, she still had a lot of work to do. But she always gave a hundred percent to everything she did. Including sucking alien cocks.

She serviced each male alien while Kigami alternated out her tentacles in probing Remy's tight holes.

"Mmm, I can't get enough of you, my gorgeous human slut!"

Remy smiled. She loved hearing she was such a hit with hot alien girls. That was totally a sci-fi nerd's dream come true.

In fact, when all five male aliens had made their cum deposits down Remy's throat, Kigami pushed Remy face first onto the floor, jumped on top of her, and ravaged her pussy and ass.

"Ohhhhh!" the sexy alien screamed. "I can't stop fucking you! Your body is divine!"

Remy squirmed beneath the titillating tentacle girl. "Please don't ever stop! I want you inside me forever!" There was something about the woman's tendrils that were so warm and comforting. They just felt right inside Remy, like her pussy and ass had been waiting her entire life for something to fill them this perfectly.

So she let Kigami pin her down and have her way with her. Remy was in so much tentacle bliss she lost track of time. They seemed to fuck for hours. They were definitely giving the gray aliens plenty of data for their studies of different species' sexual practices.

When Kigami was finally done with her, Remy panted on the floor, completely covered in tentacle cum.

"S... soooo sticky," she moaned.

"Indeed. You look delicious."

"That's nice," Remy cooed, closing her eyes. She was ready for a nice, long nap.

But the aliens had other plans. Two of the grays lifted Remy and Kigami into their arms and brought them over to the examination table. It was wider than before, big enough for both her and her new alien fuck buddy.

"They're going to experiment on us again?!"

Kigami nodded. "It seems to be their favorite thing to do."

The males laid the girls down on the table and locked their wrists and ankles into restraints.

Remy wiggled around. "Do they always tie people up during experiments?"

"I think they like seeing female sluts bound and helpless."

Remy nodded. "They're very smart aliens." She loved being bound and helpless.

"Indeed. I'm excited to get probed alongside you."

Remy smiled. "Oh, yeah! It will be nice to have a sexy girl with me this time. Being sluts together is better than being a solo slut."

"I agree."

Remy relaxed, happy to have met an alien friend who loved being fucked as much as she did.

She expected more decadent probes like the aliens' first experimentations on her.

So she was surprised when they pointed laser guns at her and Kigami's pussies.

"Ahh! What are they doing?"

"Don't worry," Kigami soothed her. "They're not weapons. The grays say they're created a new technology that emits energy beams that will stimulate female genitalia and make us have uncontrollable orgasms."

Remy gasped. "They have cum guns?"

"Something like that. It seems like we're going to become mindless, climaxing whores."

Remy gasped much louder.

Ohhhhhh fuck.

Chapter 6

One of the gray aliens inserted the cum gun into Remy's pussy.

"Oh fuck! I thought they were going to shoot us with them from across the room."

Her new, sexy, blue alien friend squirmed next to her on the examination table, receiving her own probing. "The guns have that power, but the grays tell me they're much more effective when inserted into tight pussies."

"Did they really say we have tight pussies?"

"Oh yes," Kigami replied. "I do not use hyperbole when translating sexy telepathy."

Remy smiled. She appreciated that Kigami was a woman of honor and candor. "But doesn't this mean we're going to become even bigger sluts that won't be able to stop begging to be fucked?"

"Absolutely."

"Okay, just checking." Remy wiggled as the cum gun penetrated more deeply within her. Would its powers really turn her into a raging nympho who traveled the galaxy begging every alien to treat her like their personal cum dump? She shivered at the thought: it was both scary and enticing. Fuck, when did she get so ridiculously submissive? Oh right, when aliens kidnapped her and gave her the most amazing sex of her life. And when Sam used T-69 to turn her into a robot fuck toy. And, of course, she couldn't forget Bigfoot making her realize how much she loved being fucked animal style. Kigami was the icing on the cake. No self-respecting nerd girl would refuse a hot blue alien with tentacles.

When she thought about it that way, she really had no other option than to become the galaxy's biggest whore. And she might as well do it while she possessed the youthful endurance to be fucked all day and night. Yeah, that was logical, right?

Kigami glanced at her. "You're convincing yourself why you should be an intergalactic whore, aren't you?"

Remy gasped. Both from Kigami's prescience and the phallic-gun worming into her. "How did you know?"

"I'm doing the same thing."

Remy beamed. "Yes! I knew we'd be best friends. We totally think alike! Do you want to have a sleepover at my place?"

"What is a sleep… over?"

"Oh, it's when your friend comes to your house to watch sci-fi movies all night, eat lots of junk food, and have kinky sex!"

Kigami's indigo eyes brightened. "Sleepovers sound very fun."

"They are! Oh, but the kinky sex stuff doesn't usually happen. That's just one of my fantasies."

"We will make that fantasy a reality."

Remy wanted to hug her. But, well, she was tied up. "You're the best alien girl ever!"

Kigami smiled. "That's what I was going to say to you."

The girls giggled and prepared to be blasted into orgasmic oblivion.

Once it was nice and snug in Remy's pussy, her alien doctor activated the device. A warm sensation filled her insides. It spread slowly at first, then more quickly. It got hotter and hotter. It spread through her extremities so every inch of her skin tingled. Her nipples protruded out as far as possible. Her clit burst from its hood. Her entire body felt like it was becoming one huge erogenous zone.

"Ohhhhhh fuuuuccckkk, wh… what's happening?"

"Whatever it is, it feels wonderful!" Kigami wiggled next to Remy, having been given her own sex shot.

Remy felt the familiar sensation of an oncoming orgasm, but a hundred times more powerful. Her body seized up, arching off the table in a frozen tableau of ecstasy.

And then a galactic-sized climax overwhelmed her. It was like nothing she had experienced. Her mind felt like it temporarily shut off as feelings of pure euphoria coursed through her from her fingers to her toes.

Her cum blasted out of her like something out of an alien porn video. Which was appropriate for her current setting.

She squirted like a garden hose turned on high, blasting the cum gun out of her pussy and across the room, where it clanged off the metallic wall and skidded across the floor.

"I can't stop cummmmmmmmmming!!!" she wailed, thrashing on the exam table and almost tearing her restraints off.

Kigami's tentacles spasmed rapidly, worming across Remy's body. "Th… the grays say your human body is reacting differently than they expected. The sex blast should have made you uncontrollably horny, not made you cum indefinitely."

"Wh… what?!" Remy replied, her huge gushing shooting out in various directions like it was an out-of-control sprinkler. "I thought these aliens knew what they were doing." When you meet archetypal gray aliens, you expect them to be super-smart. What the heck were they doing trying out sexy gadgets on innocent human girls? Oh right, their whole thing was experimenting on nubile women. And Remy wasn't that innocent. Though she was before meeting these guys. Silly sex aliens and their amazing gadgets that made her want to be a galactic slut.

"They believe these kind of experiments are excellent learning experiences," Kigami told her.

"Oh sure, they're… ohhhhhh fuuuuuuuuuccccckkkkk… not the ones cumming uncontrollably!" Remy's pussy was an open faucet, shooting blast after blast across the room, splattering the aliens, the walls, and the floor. She had no control over her body. Her wrist and leg restraints were the only things keeping her on the table.

"That's true. But they are enjoying watching you cum. As am I." Kigami's bright eyes were locked on Remy's waterfall.

"Ohhhhhhhhhh! Th… that's nice!" Remy's ass bounced up and down on the table with every spurt, like she was spanking herself for being such a naughty slut. "W… why isn't it making you cum?"

"I believe it's having a different effect on me. My head tendrils feel like they are about to explode." The alien girl's tentacles expanded and thrashed around, throbbing like a cock that was about to erupt.

Remy watched Kigami squirm, glad she wasn't the only one being affected by the gray aliens' sneaky sex ray.

"Ohhhhhhhhhhhhhh!" her blue friend screamed. Huge streams of thick, milky cum shot out of all four tendrils. All four of which were aimed at Remy.

"Holy shit!" Remy exclaimed, shocked at receiving such a torrent of alien cum all at once. As soon as her mouth opened, she got a blast of that cum down her throat. She swallowed Kigami's gift while continuing to have her own juicy waterworks.

The alien girl was now thrashing as much as Remy. "I... I cannot stop cumming!"

"Ohhhhhhh! G... great, but do you have to dump all of it on me?"

"Yes! No body deserves to be covered in cum as much as yours."

Remy gulped down more of Kigami's milk. She wasn't sure if her alien friend meant she deserved it because she had the hottest body on Earth or because she was the biggest slut in the galaxy. Either could be a reason to be covered in cum. But Remy took it as a compliment. It wasn't just any human girl who could say she was covered head to toe in alien tentacle cum.

"Oh fuck, thank you! Please keep cumming on me!"

Kigami granted Remy's wish. The human slut soon had a thick layer of blue covering her body. Which only intensified her own gushing. Remy had come to an important conclusion: the more aliens (or anyone really) treated her like a whore, the more she came. Being a horny slut rocked!

While the girls kept cumming, the male aliens made adjustments to their ray guns.

"Th... they're going to shoot us again?" Remy asked between moans.

Kigami nodded. "They... uhhhhhhhhh... believe they have made the proper corrections to their erotic devices."

"Ohhhhhhhh!" Remy cried. "G… great!" Remy didn't know what the kooky cosmic gun was going to do to her this time, but she didn't care. All she could think about was that her pussy was made to cum for eternity.

One of the grays shoved the nozzle of the device past her waterfall and activated it. A similar sensation flowed through Remy, but her squirting stopped. It was replaced with a building desire to be fucked. A desire like nothing she had felt before. Her pussy pulsated and burned, needing to be filled, needing to be fucked. The feeling grew and grew until Remy could no longer take it.

She yanked at her wrist restraints, needing her fingers free so she could plunge them into her desperate pussy. She didn't understand how it could be so needy after expelling gallons of cum, but that was alien technology for you. The second ray gun blast had turned her pussy into a raging inferno of desire.

And she wasn't the only one. Kigami bucked her body next to Remy, her cute aqua pussy throbbing powerfully. The grays had now tied up her tentacles so she couldn't pleasure herself or Remy. Ugh, why they'd have to be such sneaky aliens?

"Oh God, I need to be fucked so bad!" Remy wailed.

"So do I!" Kigami screamed.

The males merely stared at them with their unreadable expressions and their erect cocks. Those cocks seemed to taunt Remy. They were so close, so ready to penetrate her captured cunt. Why couldn't they just put her out of her misery and fuck her already?

"Pl… please fuck me with your huge alien cocks!" she pleaded. "I need them! I need all of them inside me!" Remy hoped they didn't interpret that to mean she wanted five alien cocks in her pussy at once. Though with the way she was feeling, she probably wouldn't have refused.

"Th… they want to observe how their devices affect us," Kigami told her. "And see how desperate we become."

Remy thrashed against her bonds. She had never wished so hard that she could turn into She-Hulk. Okay, she often wished she could turn into the muscular green hero. Who wouldn't want to be super-strong and sexy? And she was sure She-Hulk had a ridiculously tight and powerful pussy. Becoming the jump-roping superhero would have allowed her to break her restraints and pleasure herself. But she was just a normal human with no powers from gamma radiation. And, thus, she was stuck within her sexy restraints.

It was torture not having anything inside her cooch. It throbbed, telling her it was preposterous that a huge cock, dildo, or tentacle wasn't filling it, that there was no reason for it ever to be empty. Remy might have been a horny girl, but she had never felt like her pussy needed to be filled 24/7. Even she was okay giving it a break while she vegged out on sci-fi movie marathons. But her pussy's current desire was off the charts. She couldn't survive if something huge didn't get shoved it in immediately.

"Uhhhhhhhh, th… that's so not fair!" she complained. "They made us insanely horny and now they won't satisfy us."

"Indeed," Kigami agreed. "It's quite devious. But I believe they see it from a more scientific perspective."

"Screw science! I just want to be fucked!" Remy actually loved science, but when her pussy was screaming at her, sex easily topped science.

"Perhaps if we beg them appropriately, they will insert their girthy cocks in us."

"G… good idea! You're so smart." Remy looked at her male captors. "Oh sexy gray aliens, please fuck us with your huge, yummy cocks!"

They studied her, their expressions unchanging.

"That's good," Kigami told her. "But be more desperate. Tell them exactly what you're willing to do."

Remy nodded. Her alien friend was obviously very knowledgeable in these matters. Remy had a lot to learn from her. "Please shove your cocks inside me! Stick your probes in my cunt! Ram anything you want inside my slutty, alien-loving pussy!"

The males moved closer.

"It appears to be working," Kigami told her. "Keep going."

"Ohhhhhhh!" Remy gasped, raising her hips off the table so her pussy was as close to the aliens as possible. "O… okay."

Remy's hips moved of their own accord, her pussy leading them in a desperate dance of desire. "I'll be your slutty sex toy, your alien cum dump, your perfect pleasure slave!"

The grays moved even closer, their cocks quivering above Remy's prone body.

Kigami moaned as her hips copied Remy's sultry movements. "My goodness, human girls really are the ultimate sluts."

"We totally are!" Remy confessed. "Wait, I mean, th… that's only because of their sneaky sex ray. And why am I the only one screaming all this slutty stuff?"

"It's quite arousing to hear your desperate cries of desire." Kigami's head tendrils twitched at Remy like they were eager to taste her sweet juices again.

"Ohhhhh, th… that's nice. But that's not fair, Kigami. We're supposed to be sluts together. That's what friends do." Remy really hadn't done that with her friends, but she had fantasized about it. She had some hot besties.

"I see. I did not realize that was a human custom. May I make it up to you by fucking you with all my tentacles during our sleepover?"

"Yes! You can fuck me all night with them."

"It will be my pleasure. They will never leave your pussy and ass."

Remy smiled. This was going to be the best sleepover ever. And she was fully onboard with Kigami's sweet tendrils never leaving her sensitive holes. In fact, that's what she desperately wanted right now: something, anything, to be rammed up her cunt. And not just there. Her ass was burning with the same desire. The effects of the cum gun had evidently spread to her tiniest opening. So she now had two holes that needed filling. And she was going to do anything the aliens wanted to make that happen.

"Ohhhhh, Kigami, I can't take it anymore! My ass is just as desperate as my pussy. Can you please ask them to fuck me? I'll do anything they want!"

"My posterior is equally needy. I will join you in doing any debauched activity you agree to." The alien girl gazed at the grays, communicating with them telepathically.

"They have agreed to fuck us."

"Thank God!" Remy had never been happier to hear those words.

"On one condition."

Remy let out a frustrated sigh. Why did there always have to be a condition? Couldn't they just fuck the two cute naked girls who were bound on the table before them? "Okay, what is it?"

"They are curious about your offer to be a pleasure slave.

They would like you to serve as that aboard their ship and to any other alien species they encounter."

Remy froze. Which was hard to do with a crazy, throbbing pussy. The aliens wanted her to become their personal courtesan who they could fuck whenever they wanted and pass around to their alien friends?

Ohhh damn. What had she gotten herself into?

Chapter 7

"Oh my God!" Remy wailed through her horny moans. "They're serious about me becoming their pleasure slave?"

"Of course," Kigami replied, her lovely blue hips wiggling next to Remy. Both girls were beyond desperate to be fucked, thanks to the gray aliens' sneaky sex ray. "You were the one who suggested it."

Remy squirmed, her pussy and ass begging to be filled. "But that's just something you scream when you're being a big slut."

"Do many human girls scream things like that?"

"Um, well, I'm not sure." Remy hadn't been with enough girls to make assertions on behalf of the whole female race. "Probably not all of them."

"I see. So you are the biggest slut of all women on Earth."

"What?! Kigami, I didn't say that!"

"Oh. Have I misunderstood human customs again? On my world, being the biggest slut is a great honor."

Remy shivered all over. "I really need to visit your planet."

"You would be very popular there. Everyone would

want to fuck you. We would have to set up a special room where all of our species could take turns fucking you for every solar and lunar cycle."

If Remy was crazy horny before, hearing that really sent her over the edge. "Oh my goodness, does everyone want me to be their sex slave?"

"Of course. You are a beautiful and wonderfully slutty girl."

Remy beamed. "Aw, Kigami, you say the sweetest things."

"So you agree to be their pleasure slave?"

"Um, well, I'd like to, but I have a life here on Earth. I'm in college and I just started this summer job where I have to fuck sex robots."

Kigami's pretty eyes lit up. "That is a very noble occupation."

Remy giggled. Apparently, the tentacle girl's race thought anything that had to do with sex was honorable. They were an intelligent species.

"I have an idea." The sexy blue alien glanced at the grays. Remy wiggled around, wondering what they were discussing and wondering how long she could hold out before she agreed to be the sluttiest sex slave ever.

Kigami returned her attention to her fellow slut. "I suggested that you could be the official Sex Ambassador for Earth."

"A sex ambassador? Oh my God, yes! Um, wait, what would I have to do?"

"You'd have to have sex with any aliens they bring to Earth to ensure all species maintain a positive view of your planet."

"I can do that! But do they really think I'd be the best ambassador?"

"Of course. They said there is no other female on your planet who would be more desirable to be fucked by other species.

Remy blushed super-hard. "Oh my… that's so… um, thank you! That's really flattering." Did the aliens really think she was that hot? Would all other alien species actually want to fuck her that badly? Man, sci-fi encounters were a huge ego boost!

"I accept this great honor," she said solemnly. "It is my duty to ensure peaceful relations between aliens and humans by fucking every alien species that exists."

Kigami smiled. "Congratulations on your new position!"

"Thanks!" Remy had a feeling she'd be getting into a lot of new positions after meeting a bunch of new aliens.

"However, the grays have one other request."

"Okay!" After their odes to her beauty, Remy was ready to agree to just about anything.

"Anytime they visit your planet, they expect you to beam up to their ship and perform whatever sex acts they desire."

Now Remy was really trembling. "So I would be their pleasure slave after all, but just when they visit."

"Correct. You could still continue your studies and your important sex robot work."

"Deal!" Remy didn't have to think it over. Getting to live her normal nerdy life and getting to fuck aliens was a total win-win. "Will they please fuck us now?"

"Yes. But only if we agree to let them do whatever they want to us."

"Fuck, yeah! They can fuck me in every single hole and treat me like an Earth girl slut! I need my pussy and ass rammed so bad!"

"Excellent. They will be happy to hear that."

After Kigami conveyed Remy's slutty begging, the gray aliens released the restraints and flipped Remy over, pinning her arms behind her back.

They dragged her to the edge of the exam table, so her feet hit the floor and her ass was in prime probing position.

Two alien cocks entered her pussy and one pierced her ass. She tried to scream but couldn't. The triple penetration had overloaded her brain so she couldn't even process what was happening. But her pussy and ass were very clear: they wanted the alien cocks, they wanted them bad.

The effects of the sex ray must have been helping her take the two cocks in her pussy, as it seemed ridiculous that they were fitting. Of course, she did fit Bigfoot inside her, and he was beyond gigantic. Maybe she was just getting used to having her pussy and ass constantly on the verge of exploding.

Her voice finally came back, and, of course, the only thing it could utter were extremely slutty odes. “Ohhhh Goddddd, there’s so many alien cocks inside me!!!”

“There sure are,” Kigami marveled. “I’m jealous.” She wasn’t envious for long. The other two aliens bent her over next to Remy and savaged her blue pussy with their cocks. “Ohhhhhh fuuuuccckkkkkk!!”

She whimpered next to Remy, her pussy obviously just as tight as her human friend’s. But she wanted more. Specially, her ass wanted more. So she did what any self-respecting alien girl would do: she shoved two of her tendrils up her butt and fucked herself while the grays went to town on her alien cunt.

“Ohhhhh Kigami, that’s so hot!” Remy wailed, watching her new fuck buddy probe herself. “Having tentacles is so cool!”

“It… uhhhhhhhhh… is quite handy. But it is equally hot seeing three of their huge cocks filling you.”

“Ohhhhhh! I… I don’t know how I’m taking it! But I don’t want them to stop!”

“Good. For they have no intention of doing so. They’re going to pound you until you are full of their alien seed.”

“Yes! Fuck, yes, fill my pussy and ass with your alien

spunk!"

Kigami smiled. "They very much appreciate your human enthusiasm."

"I am super-enthusiastic about anything sci-fi related, especially fucking!"

Kigami laughed and moaned. "You are an enchanting human, Remy of Earth."

Remy matched her moans. Remy of Earth was a much nicer moniker than Remy the Slut, which is what T-69 called her. Of course, having three alien cocks inside her pretty much proved the sex robot was correct in his nickname for her. So maybe she could go by Remy the Slut of Earth. That could be the way she introduced herself to other aliens as the official sex ambassador for the planet. She was determined to take her new job seriously. The future of mankind could depend on her pleasing many different alien species.

Right now, there was just one alien species she needed to please: the gray aliens who were pounding her pussy and ass.

"Our lovers request we tell them how slutty we are," Kigami informed her, her face contorted in beautiful blue bliss.

"Okay!" Remy was happy to tell them anything they wanted as long as they kept fucking her. Thanks to the sex ray, the only way she felt sated was if her holes were stuffed.

"Please smash me with your huge alien cocks!" she

screamed. "I need them inside me! I need them to turn me into a slutty space whore!"

"You're very good at this," Kigami marveled. "I knew you'd be the perfect ambassador for your planet."

The sexy alien girl telepathically screamed odes to the grays. Which was totally unfair. Remy wanted to hear what slutty stuff she was saying. But she contented herself with watching the gorgeous blue body writhe in the most sensual ways, while the aliens rammed her and she pleasured the rest of her body with her tentacles.

The three aliens attending to Remy all came at once. She squealed from the sensation of thick, alien gunk pouring into her tight holes. They overflowed her, so when they pulled out, their cream streamed out of her.

Kigami suffered the same sexy fate, her pussy getting a big dose of alien cum while she shot her own juices into her ass.

Remy trembled next to her. It was so hot that her friend could jizz inside herself. What a talented alien hottie!

The aliens then took the girls to the bridge, cum dripping out of them the whole way, where they formed a circle and passed around the sluts like they were their personal playthings.

Remy was handed back and forth between the aliens: sometimes she was on her knees, sometimes on her back, and sometimes in the air being plunged onto their cocks like a sex doll. As soon as one alien was done with her, she got tossed to another, who immediately filled one of her holes. She felt like a complete fuck toy, her body existing merely to pleasure them. And she loved it! The sex ray's powers had not subsided, so she needed to be fucked constantly. She didn't care how dirty the aliens made her feel, how much of a sex slave they treated her like, she needed their huge gray cocks and needed their cum inside her as well as all over her.

Plus, she did agree to be their pleasure slave whenever they visited Earth. And orbiting the planet certainly counted. As the official sex ambassador, she'd be negligent in her duties if she didn't let them own her body.

Kigami wasn't Earth's sex ambassador, but she was eagerly allowing the grays to use her as they saw fit. Her tentacles brushed Remy's nudeness as they were passed around: sometimes the tendrils were close enough to penetrate one of Remy's open holes, adding another flavor of alien cum to the human slut's body.

The aliens made Remy blow them, jerk them off, take all their cocks in her pussy and ass. Well, not all five in the same hole, but they did delight in shoving two cocks in her very sore pussy. Remy thought they must have gotten off at shooting multiple streams of cum inside her at the same time. They may have said it was merely for scientific research, but Remy knew they were kinky fuckers.

She gazed at the brilliant swirling ball of blue below her

as she got pounded. And pounded. And pounded some more. An alien ship was a wonderful place to be fucked.

When they were done with her, she still needed more, even though she was coated head to toe in their sticky sauce.

"P… please," she begged. "I need more! I need to be fucked all the time!" She wondered if their sex blast was ever going to wear off or if she was going to become a sex slave for eternity.

"Don't worry," Kigami told her, patting her thigh and seemingly reading her mind. "The grays say the effects should wear off soon. In the meantime, they think we should fuck each other so they can acquire more data on how females mate with one another."

"Great idea! Please fuck me with all your yummy tentacles!"

Kigami grabbed Remy, shoving two tendrils in her pussy and two in her ass.

"Fuuuuuccccckkkkk, Kigami! I didn't mean stick all of them in me at once!"

"Oh come now, my lovely human slut, you took two of the alien cocks in your pussy. Surely, you can fit my tentacles. And your ass needs to know it's place, so you're going to take them and enjoy it."

"Ohhhhhhh! Y… yes, ma'am. You're so sexy when you're bossy!"

"Thank you. Now kiss me." The alien girl pressed her

lips to Remy's, and the two made out while Remy rode the writhing tentacles and surrendered to the sheer bliss of alien lesbian action.

She and Kigami made love for a long time, the grays watching and making notes. They got so excited that they stroked their cocks and jizzed all over the girls, while Remy and Kigami grinded their bodies together.

Eventually, the effects of the horny ray wore off, and Remy lay next to Kigami, covered in cum and trembling from the aftereffects of a million orgasms.

When she could finally think straight, she bolted up. "Oh, fuck!"

"What's wrong?" her cum-coated blue friend asked.

"I forgot I'm supposed to be meeting Sam for a date!" Remy leapt to her feet but then realized she was dripping in cum and had no clothes thanks to the aliens' disintegration ray.

How the heck was she supposed to go out with Sam like this?

Chapter 8

"Sam, I'm so sorry I'm late!" Remy called as she rushed into the sexy scientist's lab. She was still naked and covered in alien cum. She had the grays beam her directly outside the building so she wouldn't be even more tardy. And she knew Sam would have no problem seeing her in such a sexually-used state.

She entered the lager room with all Sam's crazy sex inventions. And was greeted with the woman's craziest invention ever.

"Remy the Slut has returned," T-69 said, stomping toward her.

"T-69! I thought you were deactivated."

"Dr. Shen has reactivated me."

"Oh, that's nice. Is Sam here?"

"Affirmative. But she is distressed due to you not arriving for your romantic rendezvous."

"Ack! I'm sorry! I didn't mean to be late, but I have a really good excuse."

"Excuses are not acceptable. You must be fucked to be put in your place." The robot seized Remy's shoulders, lifted her off the ground, and spun her around so her ass bumped against its smooth chassis.

"Wait! I thought Sam fixed you."

"Affirmative. She fixed me so I may turn you into a submissive slut."

Remy trembled. What kind of fixing was that? Oh right, the kind the kooky scientist loved.

"But I just got fucked like a million times. Can't you see all the cum all over me?"

"Yes. Your human body should always be covered in cum to signify how much of a slut you are."

"Why does everyone want me to be a slut today?"

"There is a logical answer to that. You are extremely appealing to your fellow humans, so they naturally would want to fill your holes and cover you in their seed."

"So you're saying I'm hot?"

"Your temperature is a normal 98.6 degrees."

"No, I mean... oh, never mind."

"Are you ready to be fucked?" One of T-69's huge cocks slid out of a compartment and positioned itself below Remy's pussy.

"Sure, why not? It is part of my job. And it will make Sam happy. I feel really bad about being so late."

"You may make it up to her by allowing me to turn you into my robot whore."

"Well, I've already been an alien and Bigfoot whore

today, so why not a robot whore too."

"Aliens and Bigfoot do not compute."

"Um, never mind. Just fuck me really hard, please."

"Affirmative, Remy the Slut. You are an enjoyable human to fuck."

"Thank youuuuuaaaaaaaaaaa!!" Her gratitude turned into a scream as her robot lover slammed her down on its metallic cock.

She slid down to its base and trembled. "F… fuck, I forgot how big you are."

"Dr. Shen outfitted me with an even larger prosthetic. She said my previous instruments were not big enough for a slut of your caliber."

"What?! Did she really say that?"

"I sure did!" Sam bounded into the room, slurping one of her signature strawberry smoothies. She wore a short jean skirt, sneakers, and a Back to the Future T-shirt. She looked very nerdy and very sexy.

"Sam, you're a geek girl's dream!" Remy proclaimed, wanting to jump on the scientist and make love to her.

"Thanks! You're any girl's dream." She took in Remy's wet, nude form, impaled on T-69, legs dangling off the floor.

Remy smiled at the sexy scientist. "T-69 said I had to be fucked because I was late for our date."

Sam stamped her foot. "Yeah, where were you? I put on this cute outfit for you and was waiting. I thought you stood me up."

The robot swirled its hips, worming around inside Remy.

"Fuck, T-69, it's hard to talk when you're doing that."

"Then please speak quickly. I must fuck you vigorously."

"O… okay. Sam, I swear I didn't stand you up. I've really been looking forward to our date. You look so adorable I want to tackle you, rip off your clothes, and make love to you all night long."

Sam's eyes lit up. "Ooh, really?"

"Yes! You're so sexy and geeky, I'm going to cum just looking at you."

The hot doc hopped up and down. "Yes! What an amazing superpower I have. I can make girls cum just by being nerdy."

Remy laughed. "You can definitely make this girl cum."

"Great! You're the girl I most want to make cum."

Remy smiled, then sighed. "I'm really sorry I'm late."

"Oh, don't worry. You're such a sweetheart I could never stay mad at you. And I put you through all the shenanigans with T-69."

"Oh yeah," Remy replied, still trying to adjust to the robot's mammoth cock. "I thought you fixed him."

"I did."

"But he still wants to treat me like a slut."

"Yeah, of course. I fixed him so he doesn't go on a rampage turning every woman on the planet into a slut. For now, you're the only slut he's interested in."

"What?!!"

"Isn't that great?"

"Sam!"

She slurped more of her smoothie. "But you like being a slut."

"I know, but… um, everyone's been treating me like a slut the past couple of days."

"Ooh, you lucky girl. Who else has slutted you up?"

"Uh, well…" Remy wanted to tell Sam about the aliens and Bigfoot but was desperate for robot cock. "Can I tell you after T-69 finishes fucking me?"

"Ah ha! So you do want to be a robot slut."

"It's hard not to while I'm impaled on his cock, dangling in the air, totally helpless."

"Yes! You look so fucking hot."

"And it is part of my job as your assistant, right?"

Sam smiled. "Oh yeah. It's the most important part of the job. I want you to be fucked every day you come in here."

Remy wiggled around on her current favorite cock. "Hear that, T-69? You're going to be inside my pussy a whole bunch."

"Affirmative. And inside your ass. Do not forget what an anal slut you are."

"Oh yeah," Sam added. "Remy loves it in the butt."

"Would you guys stop talking about what a slut I am and

just turn me into a slut?"

"You got it, slut! T-69, commence ultra-fucking!"

"Affirmative, Dr. Shen." The robot bypassed easy and medium mode and went right to its intense fucking level.

Remy bounced on its cock, tits jiggling, limbs flailing all over the place. "Ohhhh f… fuck!! What happened to starting with the lower modes?"

"You have proven to be a high-quality slut," the robot informed her. "It is logical to start at a higher fucking intensity."

Remy let out a series of loud moans. A high-quality slut? What was a low-quality slut? Well, if she was going to be a slut, she supposed it was better to have a higher rating.

"Ooh, good idea, T-69," Sam said as she hopped into a chair and opened her laptop on a see-through desk. "I should add a rating system for slut levels. Remy can be the benchmark for the highest rating possible."

"H… hey!" Remy replied between deep penis thrusts. "I… I'm not the biggest slut on the planet."

"Oh, do you prefer biggest slut in the galaxy?" Sam asked with a giggle.

"Uhhhhhhhhh!" Remy was making a lot of sexy noises. T-69 had learned a lot about her pussy from their previous fucking sessions. But it was probably good she was making too many erotic sounds to reply. Sam had no idea how close she came with her galactic slut remark. In fact, after serving as Sex Ambassador for Earth for a while, Remy might very well earn the title of biggest slut in the galaxy. Kigami would be so proud of her!

"I'll take that as a yes," Sam said, happily typing away at her keyboard.

Remy gazed at the horny scientist as T-69 pounded her. From the way Sam's short skirt had ridden up when she sat down, Remy could see everything underneath.

"Sam! You're not wearing any underwear." The older woman's cute pussy lips glistened at Remy, obviously getting wet from watching her young assistant get fucked.

"Oh, yeah. I got really horny thinking about our date and wanted to be all ready to have sex. Oh, um, that is, if you wanted to have sex on our first date."

Remy smiled. It was adorable how shy Sam could get when she talked about herself. She was extremely energetic talking about her inventions and Remy's slutty body but wasn't as convinced about her own hotness. Remy needed to assure her intelligent friend of her sex appeal. "Of course, I want to have sex with you! I'm been dreaming about it ever since T-69 ordered us to kiss and smashed our naked bodies together."

"Really? Oh, good! So I made the right call not wearing any panties?

"Fuck, yes! Your pussy is so cute! I love it!"

Sam shimmied on her chair, and a small puddle formed

on her seat. "Ohhhh, Remy, you're getting me so wet!"

"Woohoo! I love wet scientists." Remy bit her lip. That sounded kind of weird, but Sam knew what she meant. "Can you play with yourself while I'm getting fucked?"

"Sure!" Sam reached beneath her skirt and rubbed her slit. She had a bare, tiny pussy, and it was very sensitive. She trembled as soon as she touched it and let out an adorable squeal. Remy wanted her so bad. T-69 had fucked them simultaneously and made them cum all over each other. But they hadn't properly had sex. Remy was looking forward to making love with Sam when it was just the two of them.

"Oh fuck, I'm even more sensitive than usual!" Sam squeaked.

"Dr. Shen, that is likely due to your observation of Remy becoming a slut before your eyes." T-69 rammed Remy even harder, making her body flop around like a sex doll.

"Fuck, fuck, fuck, fuck, fuck!" the college co-ed cried. "T… T-69, I can b… barely think straight."

"Sluts do not need to think. They need to moan and cum."

That sounded logical to Remy, so she moaned and came. A lot.

"Oh my God, this is the hottest thing I've ever seen!" Sam went to town on her pussy, slamming two fingers in and out and spraying her juices every which way.

Remy couldn't take her eyes off Sam. The scientist had

her legs up on the table, fully spread, while she fucked herself savagely, her T-shirt riding up to show off her sexy stomach. Remy loved that Sam had a geeky shirt on while masturbating. Somehow that made the whole thing hotter. Remy loved smart, geeky girls. So Sam was a total turn on. It didn't hurt that the Asian woman was beautiful and sexy. And was super-fun to hang out with.

Remy thrashed on top of her robot master's cock. "T-69, please fuck me on the table so Sam gets a close-up view of all my sex faces!"

"That is an excellent idea. But you must utter the correct passphrase."

"Bend me over and ram me like the dirty slut I am until I beg to be a whore to every robot in the universe!"

"That is the correct passphrase. You are a quick learner, Remy the Slut."

Remy moan-giggled. From her past robot fuckings, she had figured out exactly what her metallic lover wanted to hear. And, apparently, T-69 wasn't the only one who enjoyed hearing it.

"Ohhh God, Remy, you're making me cum!" Sam squirted her juices in a high arc, screaming deliriously.

T-69 shoved Remy face first onto the table between Sam's legs, right into the path of the scientist's stream. Remy got it right in her mouth, and she happily lapped up her friend's cum.

Meanwhile, T-69 railed her from behind, slapping his hard body against her jiggling ass.

"Do you want it harder, Remy the Slut?"

"Ohhh fuck, yes!" Every time the robot called her that, she felt like an even bigger whore.

"Do you want me to make you cum?"

"Yesss!! Please make me cum, T-69! I need to cum so bad! I promise I'll be your whore whenever you want."

"Holy shit!!" Sam came again, incredibly turned on by Remy's submissive odes. This time she not only came all over Remy's face but also over the young slut's back and ass. Sam was a talented squirter.

"Initiating full slut mode," T-69 intoned. It rammed Remy like a jackhammer, forcing her mouth to remain open, frozen in erotic nirvana.

"Oh fuck, Remy!" Sam cried. "T-69 is completely owning you!"

"Uh… uh huh!" was the only thing Remy could get out.

"You will cum when I order you to," the robot said.

"Y… yes, sir!" she managed to reply. Remy really liked bossy robots.

He kept fucking her, teasing her with an orgasm, while Sam kept spraying her face. The horny doc seemed to be able to cum non-stop. Just another reason for Remy to date her.

"P… please let me cum, T-69!" Remy begged.

"On one condition."

"A... anything!"

"When you and Dr. Shen go on your romantic rendezvous, you must have sex in public."

"W... what?!!"

Remy stared at an equally shocked Sam. They had to fuck out in the open on their first date?

Ohhh shit.

Chapter 9

"Do you agree to have sex in public?" T-69 asked.

"We sure do!" Sam replied.

"Sam!" Remy squealed. "T-69's asking me."

"Oops, sorry. But, c'mon, it'll be fun." The hot doc was still cumming all over Remy's face.

Remy was getting pounded so hard by her robot master she was ready to agree to anything. And was eager to go on a date with the cute, geeky scientist. Why not have sex in public as part of their romantic excursion? T-69 had fucked them outside on Remy's jeep, and that was fun. It was also fun when the hunky handyman found them and gave them a good railing. Public sex was totally the way to go! "Yes! I'll totally have sex with Sam in public."

"Excellent," T-69 replied.

"Can I please cum now?" Remy knew she wasn't allowed to climax until her mechanical master gave her permission. But making her wait just meant her orgasms would be even more spectacular.

"Affirmative. You may cum. I will join you and fill you with my robot seed."

Remy loved robot seed and squirmed on the table as T-69 pumped its fake fluids into her. She expelled her own with gratifying screams, beyond happy she could finally let loose the orgasms that had welled up within her.

T-69 had a lot of cum to dump into her. Remy was used to that so patiently took it all, staring at Sam's waterworks, which slowed from a geyser to a trickle.

Remy panted on the table, eking out a few more glops. "Ohh boy, that was a good fucking."

"Affirmative. It is always good to fuck you, Remy the Slut."

"You really like calling me that, don't you?"

"That is your name. Why would I address you as anything else?"

Sam giggled uncontrollably.

Remy stuck her tongue out at the horny scientist. "It's because of your programming it calls me that."

"I know. Isn't it great?"

"Yeah, great." T-69 gave Remy one last slam with its cock, instantly making her have another huge orgasm, and her sarcasm quickly changed to submission. "I mean, yes, it's fucking great!"

"That is better," the robot said. "Remember, you should always be a submissive slut when my cock is inside you."

"Y… yes, T-69. I won't forget!"

Sam squirted again. "God, I love it when my inventions

dominate you."

"You're a sexy menace!" Remy screamed in ecstasy.

"Better than being an unsexy menace."

"Th... that's true. Can we go on our date now?"

"Sure! But we have to think of someplace where we can have sex in public."

"Oh, right. I agreed to that, didn't I?"

"You sure did!"

"You will agree to anything when I am pounding your pussy," T-69 added helpfully.

"Um, yup." Remy couldn't disagree. She was captive to the dominating robot when he was inside her.

"Let's go to the mall," Sam suggested. "I bet we can find lots of public places to have sex there."

"We're doing it in public in multiple places?" Remy asked in surprise.

T-69 vibrated inside her pussy. It had left its monster cock within her womb, making sure she knew she had to obey its commands. "That is an excellent idea, Dr. Shen."

"I'm full of good ideas. Especially when it comes to sex!"

Remy giggled. She loved Sam's enthusiasm. "Okay, the mall it is. But, um, I don't have any clothes."

"No problem," Sam replied. "You can go naked."

"What?!"

"Just kidding! Though no one would complain seeing your hot, cum-covered body."

Remy blushed. She was covered in a lot of cum. And would certainly make a scene if she went outside without cleaning off.

"I have some extra clothes you can borrow," Sam told her.

Remy let out a sigh of relief. She might be willing to have sex in public, but she wasn't ready to go full nudist.

T-69 finally eased its cock out of her and helped her stand. The robot might love dominating her pussy, but it could still be sweet. "Be sure to document your public sex," it told them.

Remy clutched its metallic arms. "What?! We have to take pictures of us having sex?"

"Negative. You may also take a video if you prefer."

"Ack! That's even more embarrassing."

Sam wrapped her arms around Remy's waist. "Don't worry, T-69. I'll make sure to get plenty of evidence for you that our girl's a huge public whore."

"Hey!" Remy protested. "You better be in these pictures and videos too."

"Oh, I will. I want to be a big public whore with you!"

"You're a very strange scientist."

"Strange scientists are sexy!"

Remy giggled. Well, this strange scientist certainly was. "I can't argue with that."

"Let's get you cleaned up!" Sam yanked Remy into the

bathroom, which included a shower. The scientist stripped out of her clothes and thoroughly soaped up the young co-ed. Remy squirmed and gasped from how Sam touched her and returned the favor, washing the scientist's sexy parts.

They toweled off in front of T-69, knowing the robot would enjoy ogling their wet, naked bodies. It told them it would make them much wetter the next time it fucked them. Robots could be very kinky.

Sam led Remy into a back room where she kept extra clothes and toiletries for her all night mad scientist sex sessions.

Remy slipped into a Wonder Woman T-shirt and ultra-tight jean shorts. They probably fit fine on Sam, but Remy had curvier hips and a juicier booty, a booty that threatened to burst free from the shorts at any moment.

"You need to wear those shorts all the time," Sam told her.

"But you can almost see my ass."

"Exactly!"

Remy rolled her eyes. Though secretly knew she was going to wear the shorts for Sam all the time. She liked turning the older woman on.

They said their goodbyes to T-69 and promised to be its sex slaves when they returned. It went into power saving mode, wanting to be at maximal capacity to fuck its two favorite sluts.

They jumped in Remy's jeep and took off for the mall.

Remy basked in the warm sun as the wind whipped her hair. There was nothing like driving on a beautiful summer day with a cute girl in the passenger seat.

That cute girl still wasn't wearing panties. She hiked her skirt up, teasing Remy by almost revealing her bare lips.

"Sam! Don't distract me while I'm driving. Your pussy is too cute!"

"Aw, thanks! But, okay, sorry. Isn't it fun not wearing panties?" Sam had insisted Remy go commando too. Remy felt naughty having nothing on underneath Sam's tiny shorts.

"Yup. I might have to throw away all my underwear."

"Great idea! Except keep your slutty thongs. I want to see you in those."

"How do you know I have slutty thongs?"

"With an ass like yours, it'd be criminal not to."

Remy blushed. She made a mental note to model all her skimpy underwear for Sam.

They pulled into the mall parking lot. Remy lived in a small town, so there was only one mall. But it was a good one with plenty of fun stuff to do.

She unhooked her seatbelt and went to open the door.

"Wait!" Sam cried. "We have to fuck first."

"What?!"

"Remember, we're supposed to have sex in multiple

locations. This is a good place to start."

"But we're out in the open!"

"Duh, that's what makes it public sex."

"Oh, right. But, my jeep is really out in the open." Unlike a car, there wasn't much hiding the two girls from view.

"That just makes it more exciting. Scooch over here." Sam moved her seat back, then dropped to her knees on the floor.

Remy hopped into the passenger seat, and Sam put her hands on her young lover's bare legs. She caressed them, working her way up to Remy's shorts.

"Ohhh, that feels nice," Remy cooed."

"It will feel even nicer when I get these shorts off."

"But I'll be naked!"

"Yup. How else am I going to fuck you?"

Remy squirmed in her seat. Sam made a good point, but there was way too much pedestrian traffic for Remy's liking. "I'm just nervous to do it in public."

"We did it in public outside my lab."

"But that was in an abandoned strip mall. There are way more people here."

"Yeah. Exciting, right?"

"Umm..." Remy had actually had sex outside multiple times thanks to Bigfoot. He fucked her all over the place in the woods. But no one else was around. It was more nerve-wracking knowing anyone could walk by at any moment.

But also more thrilling. And it was hard to resist Sam. She gazed up at Remy with her cute face and bright eyes, gently rubbing Remy's soft skin.

"Okay, let's do it!" Remy exclaimed.

"Yes! You're my kind of girl. Let's get you stripped." Sam unbuttoned and unzipped the shorts she had loaned to Remy but had trouble pulling them down. "Oh man, it's hard to get these off."

"I'm sorry! My booty's too big."

"Are you crazy? Your booty's the most scrumptious thing I've ever seen. It's the perfect size and don't you forget it."

"Oh, o… okay. Thanks!" Remy loved how sweet Sam was. And the hot doc's ode to her ass just meant Remy was going to let Sam do whatever she wanted to her.

"But you're getting lots of spankings later for disparaging your butt."

"Yes, please!" Remy loved spankings. Even more so after being strapped to Sam's spanking machine and getting disciplined by T-69 and the aliens.

"Shimmy your hips," Sam instructed, tugging the shorts down her lover's body.

"Yes, ma'am!" Remy shimmied. She had gotten a lot of practice doing that lately. When Bigfoot, aliens, robots, and sexy scientists fucked her, she couldn't help but shimmy.

"Ma'am?" Sam replied. "Oh no, I'm an old lady taking

advantage of a young college student. I've turned into a cougar!" She stopped tugging, with Remy's shorts midway down her thighs.

Remy clasped Sam's hands. "Sam! You're not a cougar. You're only 30 years old."

"But I'm ten years older than you."

"So what?"

"Isn't it weird?"

"No. You're beautiful and sexy and fun. I like that you're older. It makes me feel like I have to submit to you and do whatever you say."

Sam's eyes brightened. "Really?"

"Yup. That's why I called you ma'am. I need to obey your sexy commands."

"Holy shit, yes! You can call me ma'am as much as you want. I love it when you obey my sexy commands."

Remy smiled and kissed her. "Plus you could easily pass for a college student."

"I could?"

"Yup."

Sam smooched Remy a bunch more. "You're the sweetest girl ever. And the best assistant ever. Now let me at that pussy!"

Remy giggled as Sam yanked her shorts the rest of the way down.

The scientist leaned in and let her breath fall across

Remy's bare lips.

"Ohhh," Remy gasped.

"Wow," Sam marveled. "You're already wet."

"It's hard not to when I'm around you."

Sam beamed up at her. "You're getting the best pussy licking ever!" She eased her tongue along Remy's slit. Remy spasmed, her lips instantly recognizing Sam's gentle touch and begging for more.

Sam gave her more, licking up, down, and around Remy's pulsating pussy. Remy squirmed, desperate to be penetrated but also trying to maintain some composure. No one had walked super-close to them, but there were people in nearby rows heading to and from their cars.

Remy gripped the seat as she tried to control her breathing.

"Uh uh," Sam scolded. "I want you to be loud for me." She flicked at Remy's clit, making it shoot out of its hood.

"S… Sam!" Remy gasped. "I… I can't be too loud. Everyone will hear me."

"Everyone should know what a slut you are." Another clit flick. And another loud gasp from Remy.

"Ohh God, I… I need you to fuck me so bad!"

"You got it!" Sam plunged into Remy's pussy, giving her a good tongue thrashing.

Remy grabbed the headrest, trying in vain to control her moans. Sam was very talented at pussy excavating. Remy knew her older lover was going to mine her for all her sweet juices.

Her butt bounced off the seat, her hips forced to do a dance of decadent delight.

Sam looked up at Remy while she tongue fucked her, keeping eye contact the whole time. Remy found that both hot and romantic. She wanted Sam so bad. She wanted to unleash her girl juices into the sexy scientist's mouth.

She knew she was about to get her wish: her orgasm was rushing to its climax, welling up inside her where it would be forced to shoot out at any moment.

And that's, of course, when a group of Remy's friends came sauntering toward her jeep.

Remy gasped, both from shock and from what Sam was doing to her pussy.

She was so fucked.

Chapter 10

"Oh my God, my friends are coming!" Remy told Sam in alarm.

"Actually, you're cumming," the sexy doc replied, watching Remy's fluids leak out of her. It had been bad timing that she made Remy orgasm just as her friends walked out of the mall.

Luckily, those friends hadn't spotted Remy yet. But she had to move fast.

She ducked down and climbed across the seats. Her climax made her slip, and she fell right onto her stick shift, her pussy getting impaled by it. "Ohhhhhhh fuck!!!"

Remy struggled to get off her gear shift, which surprisingly fit very snugly inside her. She knew her friends must have heard her ecstatic cry and would be able to see her at any moment.

Sam hopped from the floor to the passenger seat, echoing Remy's shriek. "Ohhhhhhh fuck!!!"

Remy bucked her hips, finally getting free of the stick shift, and opened her door, tumbling out the other side of the jeep onto the pavement.

She kicked the door shut just as she heard a cute voice ask, "Are you okay?" It was her friend Lily, who she had last seen after the sci-fi movie marathon and just before she had her own sci-fi sex marathon with the aliens.

She peeked under her jeep: Lily's feet were clad in sandals while those next to her were adorned with beat-up sneakers, which meant Ryan was with her. Remy could identify all her friends by their footwear. She didn't recognize the third pair of feet. Were Lily and Ryan cheating on her with a new bestie? Geez, a girl spends a couple of days having sex with aliens, robots, and cryptids and her friends start hanging out with new people.

"Oh, yeah, I'm fine," Sam replied to Lily. "I was just so excited that I found all these singles in the glove compartment." The sound of dollar bills rippling through Sam's fingers carried through the air.

Remy let out a sigh. Sam was covering for her cum-induced scream. What a nice scientist.

"Wait, isn't this Remy's jeep?" Lily asked.

"Why does she have so many dollar bills in her glove compartment?" Ryan queried.

"She loves going to strip clubs!" Sam told them.

Remy gasped. What a naughty scientist! And where did she get all those dollar bills? Remy didn't keep any money in her car. Was Sam stashing them in her bra? Up her cute butt? She was definitely full of surprises.

"Why didn't she invite me?" Lily pouted.

"I wouldn't say no to a strip club," Ryan added.

"Me either," a sultry voice agreed. Who was this hot-sounding mystery woman? And when did her friends get so into watching girls strip? Were they as kinky as Remy? Could she tell them about the aliens and Bigfoot tying her up and fucking her like a slutty sex toy?

She inched her shorts up her legs, so her bare butt wasn't sticking out. She was still cumming, but she would just have to soak the shorts she borrowed from Sam. She stuck the top of her shirt in her mouth to muffle her sexy moans.

She huddled on the ground next to her jeep, listening and watching the three pairs of feet. When people walked by on her side of the vehicle, she pretended to check her tire pressure, not that car maintenance usually involved a girl writhing around on the ground. But after Sam's attack on her pussy, she couldn't help but have a bunch of fantastic orgasms.

"How do you know Remy?" Lily asked.

"She's helping me with my research to make some extra money over the summer," Sam replied.

"Oh good!" Remy's cute friend said. "I'm glad she found a job."

"What are you researching?" mystery girl asked.

"Sex!"

Remy gasped again. Dammit, why did Sam have to

reveal all these details? Now her friends would think she was a nymphomaniac. That wasn't necessarily an incorrect assessment, but Remy had a reputation as a nice girl. Could she be both nice and naughty? Well, why not? Sam was naughty but also sweet. That's why Remy was so attracted to her.

Lily stomped her foot. "What?! I can't believe she didn't tell me."

Remy winced. She usually told her best friend everything but hadn't had time with the non-stop sex sessions.

"That's my fault," Sam replied. "She just started, and I've kept her really busy. She let me borrow her jeep to run some errands while she's back at the lab hard at work."

"That makes sense," Lily conceded. "She always works hard in school. Well, can you tell her to text me when you get back? I miss her cute butt."

Remy peeked at her butt, which was still squirming around from her climaxes. She didn't know Lily thought it was cute. What an awesome bestie! And Lily had certainly seen her naked plenty of times during sleepovers. Not that the two had ever done anything sexual. Well, except practice kissing when they were thirteen. Who else was Remy going to learn to kiss from?

"Will do!" Sam called as the trio walked off.

Remy watched from beside the jeep until Ryan's car drove away.

She exhaled and had her last, best orgasm. "Thank God!!!"

Sam peeked over the driver's side door. "How you doing down there?"

"Great! I came so many times."

The sexpot scientist smiled. "Look like you got my shorts nice and soaked." She helped Remy into the jeep, sitting the younger woman on her lap.

Remy nestled into Sam, still trembling from the post-orgasm tremors. "Yeah, sorry. You're a very good pussy licker."

"Thank you! And don't worry, I've cum in those shorts lots of times. Most recently thinking about you."

"Wait, really?"

"Yup, after you left that first day, I masturbated to videos of T-69 fucking you."

"Sam!"

"What? It was for research purposes."

Remy wrinkled her nose. "Yeah, right."

"I promise I won't show them to anyone else. But they're so hot, I can't help but fuck myself when I watch them."

"Oh, th… that's nice." Remy liked that her fuckable body was irresistible to her new, sexy boss.

"It sure is!"

Remy smiled and smooched Sam. "Thanks for covering for me with my friends. I would have been so embarrassed if they saw me having an orgasm."

"Why? You would have just made them rip their clothes off and fuck until they had huge orgasms too."

"Sam! Those are my friends."

"Yup, and they're total horndogs."

"How can you tell?"

"I'm a sex scientist, remember?"

"Oh, right. But, um, don't tell them about T-69 fucking me, okay?"

Sam patted Remy's leg. "Don't worry, it will be our little secret."

Remy smiled again. She liked having sex secrets with Sam. "But where did you get so many dollar bills? And why did you tell them I love going to strip clubs?"

"Don't you?"

"Um, I don't know. I've never been."

"What?! I have to take you. Or even, better, have you perform."

"I can't strip for people!"

"You're going to strip for me and T-69."

"I am?"

"Yup. I already talked it over with him. He thinks it's a great idea."

Remy rolled her eyes. Of course, he did. The robot existed to make Remy feel like a submissive slut. Though she realized this was the first time she and Sam referred to the sexy creation as a male. But she supposed that made sense. She had gotten to know T-69 so well, it would be weird to keep calling the robot "it."

"So that's why I have all these singles." Sam waved the stack of money in Remy's face. "We're going to shove them down your G-string while you prance around for us."

"But I don't know how to prance."

"Oh please, I bet you're a great dancer."

"Well…" It was true Remy loved to dance, and her friends said she was good. But that didn't mean she knew how to strip-dance.

"Aha! I knew it!" Sam tickled Remy's sides.

"Ahhhhhh! Sam, stop!" Remy was very ticklish and would easily submit to the older woman if she kept it up. Actually, she would submit to her anyway. Sam was so hot!

"Only if you agree to strip for me and T-69."

"Um, okay, but I don't have a G-string."

"What do you think we're here for?"

"You want me to try them on in front of you?"

"Hell, yeah. I need to see the one that makes me cum the most."

Remy envisioned herself modeling G-strings in a dressing room while Sam salivated over her barely-clad body and slapped and pinched her ass cheeks. "I will model the skimpiest underwear ever for you!"

Sam beamed. "That's the spirit!"

Remy wiggled on her lover's lap, her mind wandering to another illicit scenario: one of her dancing topless while human and robot fingers shoved dollar bills in her G-string. Oh boy, that was hot. She had no idea she wanted to strip so badly.

They shared some sweet kisses then hopped out of the jeep.

"I better buy some new shorts too, since, I, um, soaked yours so much."

"You can soak my shorts anytime, sweetie. Let's go shopping!" Sam swatted Remy on the butt, propelling her toward the mall entrance.

Remy smiled and took the older woman's hand. Sam was such a goofball, but Remy loved goofballs.

They hit Bouncy Boutique first. The store had fun and cute clothes, even though people joked that the "Bouncy" part of their name came from how their tops emphasized girls' bouncing boobs. Remy had no problem with that. She liked watching girls' boobs bounce, especially Sam's. The scientist didn't have especially large breasts, but they were frisky and moved sensually whenever she walked. And they felt great in Remy's hands. She needed to fondle the hot scientist again as soon as possible.

They chose a bunch of outfits and a bunch of G-strings. Besides everyday wear, the boutique also had a naughtier section. That was Sam's favorite.

She yanked Remy into one of the small dressing rooms and had her stripped in an instant. Remy was impressed with how quickly the scientist could get a girl's clothes off. Remy found herself hoping Sam would strip her every time they got together. She liked being naked around her geeky, new friend.

Sam made Remy model every single G-string for her. Remy had worn thongs before but never anything this skimpy. On Sam's instruction, she posed in different positions and shook her tush.

Sam took out a notepad and pencil from her tote bag and jotted down info for each G-string.

"Sam, what are you doing?" Remy asked, peeking over her shoulder while she modeled aqua underwear.

"Your butt looks so scrumptious in each one, it's going to be hard to decide a winner. So I'm making detailed notes on your ass."

"Detailed notes on my ass?"

"Sure. There are important categories like how each G-string affects the look of your ass in terms of firmness, jiggle, bounciness, and amount of exposed flesh.

Remy tingled. She had no idea this much work went into choosing the right G-string. "You're a very dedicated scientist."

"Yup. Especially when it comes to your butt."

"My butt is blushing!" Remy said, giggling.

"I'll get it to blush." Sam spanked Remy multiple ties, making the young woman's cheeks red.

"Ack! You're such a good spanker. But we can't be too loud."

"Well, that might be a problem, because we need to have sex in here."

"We do?"

"Of course. Remember, T-69 said we had to have sex in multiple places."

"Actually, you suggested that and he agreed it was a good idea."

"I'm full of good ideas."

"I'm full of T-69's cum!" Remy blurted before she realized what she had said. "Eek! I've become a slutty confessor."

Sam spun Remy around and pulled their tits together. The scientist's hands roamed down Remy's back until she found her favorite ass and squeezed. "I love it when you confess slutty things. And you are really good at giving robot blowjobs."

"Ohhh yeah." Remy remembered how much artificial cum T-69 shot down her throat. And shot into her pussy and ass. He was an expert at filling her holes.

"Now that you're in the mood and your pussy's nice and wet, let's get this G-string off you and dildos in you." Sam slid the thin fabric down Remy's legs, leaving her completely naked.

"You brought dildos with you?"

"You know it! What do you think I have in this bag?"

"Um, cool geeky stuff?" Remy never left home without nerdy paraphernalia: her *Spy x Family* key chain, her *Sailor Moon* backpack, and her plush Wicket the Ewok who rode on her dashboard.

"You're right! Meet golden rod." Sam pulled out a large, golden dildo. Remy got the joke immediately. Han Solo called C3P0 "golden rod" in *Star Wars*. Sam had obviously named her sex toy after her love for the galaxy far, far away. No wonder Remy adored this girl.

"I want to be fucked by golden rod!" Remy exclaimed. If there was one way to get in Remy's pants, it was to mix geekiness with sex. Sam totally got her.

Sam pressed the ridiculously large sci-fi-named toy against Remy's lips.

Remy gasped. She had always wanted to be fucked in a dressing room with a dildo named after one of her favorite geeky characters. Yup, she had very specific fantasies.

She closed her eyes as she got penetrated, hoping this would turn her into a sexy Jedi.

May the Force be with her!

Chapter 11

Sam pushed Remy against the wall of the dressing room as the golden dildo penetrated the sexy co-ed.

Remy clasped her lover's shoulders. "S... Sam, it... it's so big!"

"I like seeing your cute cooch stuffed." Sam shoved it in farther. "You like it too, don't you, sweetie?"

"Y... yes," Remy confessed in a desperate gasp. The sci-fi named sex toy was forcing her pussy to expand almost to its limit.

Remy gazed at the Asian woman dominating her. She was so beautiful. Remy knew she'd give her body to Sam anytime the scientist demanded. And Remy hoped she'd demand it a lot.

Sam kept probing Remy's tightness, making the young woman's moans increase.

Remy buried her mouth in Sam's neck, trying to muffle her lustful cries.

"You're doing such a good job taking golden rod," Sam told her cheerfully. "You're a true sci-fi slut!"

"Th... thank you!" Remy gasped. If only Sam knew how

true that was. Remy was probably the greatest sci-fi slut on Earth. Unless those aliens were zipping across the globe, fucking hot girls of all different nationalities. They better not be. Oops, Remy didn't realize she was jealous of the aliens sleeping with other girls. Well, she was fine with them fucking Kigami, her sexy, tentacle-haired friend. But she liked being the only human girl in their harem. She was the official Sex Ambassador for Earth after all. Therefore, she should be their main human fuck toy. She'd have to make sure to be really submissive next time they abducted her to show them no other Earth girl could satisfy them like she could.

But she had her own Earth girl to satisfy: Sam had gotten the gold sex toy fully in Remy's cunt. Remy squirmed, trying to adjust to the beast stuck inside her.

"Fuck, I'm stuffed!" she told Sam.

"You sure are!" The scientist gazed eagerly at Remy's engorged pussy. "You look so hot."

"Really?"

"Yup. You should have a huge dildo in your pussy twenty-four hours a day."

"With how you and T-69 have been fucking me, I feel like I have."

"Isn't it great?"

Remy giggled, which made golden rod tickle her insides. "Oh yeah."

"Okay, time to fuck the shit out of this tight pussy," Sam proclaimed. She grabbed the end of the dildo, preparing to ram it in and out of Remy's tight center.

"Sam, I'll be too loud. You now how noisy I get when you fuck me."

"Oh yeah, you're one vocal slut. I love it!"

Remy blushed. Lots of people and creatures had been pleased with her vocal sluttiness lately. "What if someone hears me?" There hadn't been anyone else in the dressing room area when they entered, but that didn't mean they'd be alone forever. And Remy's cries could easily carry to the rest of the store.

"Well, then they'll probably think Remy the Slut is getting fucked hard in the dressing room."

"Hey! That's T-69's name for me."

"Aha! So you do like it when he calls you that."

"Um, maybe. It makes me feel really slutty."

"Like you have to do whatever he commands?"

"Uh huh." Remy thought back to all the dominating orders the robot had given her, and how she had agreed to every single one of them, no matter how submissive it made her feel.

"Then it's a really good name," Sam concluded.

"Well, that's logical," Remy conceded. "Okay, I'm Remy the Slut, and I need to be fucked!"

"And I'm Sam the Sexpot, and I need to smash this

pussy!" She immediately began pounding Remy with golden rod.

And Remy immediately felt like she was in her favorite space fantasy universe. "Use the Force on my pussy!" she begged.

Sam sped up. "Ooh, that's so hot. Say more sexy Star Wars stuff."

"O... okay!" Mixing *Star Wars* and sex was Remy's dream come true. "Um, I'm fluent in over six million forms of cumming!"

"You sure are! Give me more!" Sam seemed to really enjoy Remy's slutty version of their sci-fi favorite.

"I made the Kessel Cum Run in less than twelve parsecs!"

"Oh fuck, you're making me so hot!" Somehow Sam stripped off all her clothes while still ramming Remy, effortlessly switching hands as she tore off her garments. Remy's potential new girlfriend was apparently sexually ambidextrous.

Sam slammed Remy as hard as possible. The huge dildo squished in and out of Remy's wet folds, plumbing her for her most intimate fluids.

"Give me one more sexy line, then cum for me, you sweet slut!" Sam ordered in that chipper way of hers.

Remy liked being a sweet slut so was happy to comply. "Do or do not. There is no try when it comes to being a slut!"

She came as soon as the words left her mouth. She couldn't quote Yoda while being fucked and not have an epic orgasm. If she hadn't cum, she wouldn't be able to call herself a true geek girl.

Sam pressed her lips to Remy's, enveloping her moans in a passionate kiss. She whipped golden rod out, letting Remy loose her fluids all over the dressing room floor.

Remy was embarrassed about making such a mess, but the Force was strong within her pussy.

Sam held Remy's convulsing body and continued to kiss her, rubbing her pussy against Remy's so she could get the college student's juices all over her.

Sam lowered them to the seat built into the wall and brushed Remy's hair out of her face. "Can you make sexy sci-fi references every time I fuck you?"

Remy smiled. "I... I'll do my best."

Sam smooched her. "You are one cool girl, Remy Alvarez."

"You are one sexy scientist, Samantha Shen."

"It's time this sexy scientist experiments some more on your sexy body. On your knees, sweetie." She yanked Remy off the seat onto the floor.

"You're going to fuck me again?" Remy asked.

"Of course. You think I'll ever get tired of making love to you?"

"I hope not!" Remy blurted.

Sam giggled and twisted Remy's arms behind her back. "Let's get you tied up and get two dildos in you this time."

Remy gasped. She knew what that meant: both her pussy and ass were getting filled. As Sam's assistant, she felt it was only proper to go along with whatever experiments the scientist thought up, even if they were taking place in a dressing room. Remy imagined all the patrons in the store coming in and gazing at her naked, wet body, her holes stuffed with dildos, completely at Sam's mercy. Dammit, she wanted everyone to know what a huge fucking whore she was!

Yikes! What was she saying? She was really becoming a sex fiend. Maybe everyone didn't have to know she was a huge whore. But sexy scientists, robots, aliens, and creatures like Bigfoot certainly could.

Sam used the G-strings to tie Remy's arms nice and snug. Remy didn't realize sexy underwear had so many uses.

The horny scientist knelt in front of Remy, spreading her bound lover's legs. "Golden rod is eager to get inside this pussy again."

Remy tingled. "My pussy loves golden rod!"

Sam smiled and slid the golden monster all the way in to Remy's quivering cunt.

"Oh God, it feels so good!" Remy gasped, her entire body shaking.

"It'll feel even better when I get this in your butt." Sam

removed a tear drop shaped anal plug from her bag.

"Yikes!" Remy couldn't take her eyes off it.

"What? You said you love getting your ass fucked."

"Yeah, but it... it's so big!"

"Duh, that's how we make you an even bigger butt slut."

"Oh. Okay, that makes sense." Remy did want to become a bigger butt slut. After the aliens and T-69 rammed her hiney so much, she had become a little obsessed with her ass being filled.

"I knew I hired the right girl." Sam scooted behind Remy and placed the tip of the toy against the college student's tiny opening.

She pressed it upward, breaking Remy's barrier.

"Uhhhhhhh!" Remy groaned. Anal piercings made her feel particularly slutty.

Sam struggled to get the large plug farther in. "Damn, you're so tight."

"S... Sam, it's not going to fit!" Remy wailed.

"Trust me, sweetie, it'll fit. Just push back. We'll get it in this slutty butt of yours."

Remy forced her hips down as Sam pressed up. Every inch of penetration spread her ass more than she thought possible. She winced, groaned, and gasped, wondering if her poor booty would survive the sinful sex toy.

After a lot of work, when they got it almost all the way in, Remy's ass suddenly sucked the final part of it inside her.

She couldn't decide if it was more painful or pleasurable, and her throat couldn't decide what kind of noise to make, so she opened her mouth in a voiceless scream.

She wiggled around, trying to adjust to the new resident in her ass. The only part of it not inside her was its circular base, which would let Sam pull it in and out as she saw fit.

"Oh wow, your ass looks so hot!" Sam exclaimed. "It keeps expanding and contracting, trying to figure out how to deal with the huge toy."

"Ohhhhh, I know!" Remy squealed. "I can barely think straight with it inside me."

"Great. I don't want you thinking about anything except being my slut."

"O... okay. I like being your slut." In fact, Remy loved being the older woman's slut. She was going to do whatever kinky thing Sam requested. She hoped Sam would take her home tonight and make her a sex slave and then cuddle with her in the morning.

Sam walked around to face Remy, admiring her handiwork. "You look beyond scrumptious."

Remy stared up at her lover. She knelt with her legs spread, golden rod in her pussy, a huge anal plug in her ass, and her arms tied behind her with sexy underwear. She felt like a complete fuck toy and completely at Sam's mercy. The sexy doc really knew how to dominate women.

Sam backed up against the wall, rubbing her adorable

pussy lips. "Come lick my cunt," she told Remy.

Remy began walking on her knees, but Sam held up a hand.

"No crawling, sweetie," she told Remy. "Hop over to me."

"But that's going to ram the sex toys even farther into me."

"Exactly." Sam had a big smile on her face. What a devious little scientist.

Remy started hopping. Each hop was amazing agony, the dildo and anal plug destroying her pussy and ass.

By the time she reached Sam, she was trembling and breathing hard.

Sam knelt and hugged her. "Doing okay, sexy pants?"

"Y... yeah," Remy replied, thinking she would wear any kind of slutty pants Sam wanted. Or even better, no pants at all. She was getting used to being nude a good portion of each day. "It's just... I feel like I'm your sex toy."

"Yes!" Sam cheered. "Mission accomplished."

Remy giggled. "You're one weird scientist."

"And you're one sexy slut. Now, eat me out!" She stood back up and plastered Remy's lips to her pussy.

Remy licked Sam's sweetness, happy to pleasure the naughty and nice scientist.

She flicked up and down Sam's slit before penetrating her, tasting her warm and gooey center. Remy loved going down on girls: she loved the sounds they made, the way their hips shimmied, the sweet fluids they dripped into her mouth.

Sam tugged Remy's hair, indicating she wanted her slut to look at her. The scientist held a remote in her hand and pressed a button on it.

The dildo and anal plug spurred into action, vibrating within Remy's pussy and ass.

Remy squealed, not realizing the sex toys had those kind of remote capabilities. But she should have known: Sam never did anything basic when it came to sex.

She moaned into Sam's lips and leaked slutty juices out of her pussy. She was in a state of never-ending bliss. She had no control over her pussy and ass: Sam could vibrate them as hard as she wanted. So Remy tried to focus on pleasing her mistress, wanting Sam to cum all over her face and down her throat.

Sam's hips danced, and her moans got louder. Remy knew she had her lover on the precipice of an epic orgasm.

And that's when there was a loud knock on the dressing room door.

"What's going on in there?" a female voice called out.

Remy froze. Oh shit, they were so busted.

Chapter 12

The door flew open, revealing an elegant woman dressed in a fashionable top and skirt, her shapely legs on full display.

She was 40 years old but had a timeless beauty, a deep tan covering her entire body. Remy knew this because this was her neighbor, Kiarra Costa, who was the manager at Bouncy Boutique.

The gorgeous woman had been born in southern Italy but went to college in the U.S. and stayed there afterwards. Her accent wasn't as strong as it used to be, but it was still sexy as hell. As was she. Kiarra was total MILF material. Remy and every other horny teen in the neighborhood had a huge crush on her growing up. Heck, Remy still had a huge crush on her. Kiarra seemed to be just as beautiful now as when Remy was a kid. Remy fondly remembered the skimpy bikinis Kiarra wore at pool parties, which is how Remy knew she was tan all over. A wonderful, sexy tan that Remy wanted to examine up close.

Oops, she hoped she wasn't drooling. Kiarra had been her first crush, so it was hard not to think naughty stuff about her. Especially when Remy was tied up and cumming.

Because that's exactly what she did when the Italian entered. The vibrating toys in her pussy and ass already had Remy on the edge. Kiarra's appearance pushed her over that edge, making her gush her slutty college fluids.

"Ohhhhhhh fuck!!" she wailed.

"Ohhhhhhh fuck!!" Sam echoed, squirting all over Remy's face.

"Remy, what are you doing?" Kiarra asked in shock.

"Ahhhhhh! I'm… I'm cumming!" Remy squirmed on her knees, her waterworks shooting out between her legs. "I'm sorry, Miss Costa, I can't stop!"

"Me either!" Sam shrieked, yanking Remy's hair so the young slut had to take the full blast of the scientist's pussy right in the face.

Remy let out all her juices, then panted on her knees, cum dripping off her body as she stared up at her neighbor. She was so embarrassed Kiarra had seen her climax uncontrollably. And embarrassed that the older woman was eyeing the two big vibrators rumbling inside Remy's pussy and ass.

"Sam, shut these off!" Remy told her mischievous boss.

The Asian cutie was leaning against the wall, looking very satisfied with how Remy had eaten her out. "Oh, right." She snatched the remote and turned off the dual sex toys.

"Miss Costa, I can explain," Remy said desperately.

The older woman gazed up and down Remy's wet body. "Really?"

Remy did a once over of her cum-covered flesh. "Um, okay, I can't explain. Sam tied me up and fucked the shit out of me. But we're really sorry!"

"I'm not sorry," Sam said unhelpfully. "I love watching you cum."

"Sam!" Remy scolded her before turning back to Kiarra. "Please don't arrest us, Miss Costa!"

Kiarra smiled. "Remy, first off, I've told you a million times to call me Kiarra."

"Oops, sorry Miss Cos… I mean, Kiarra."

"Second, why would I have you arrested?"

"Um, because we had sex in public and drenched your dressing room?"

"That's a rite of passage of any young woman," the elegant beauty replied. "Besides, I've been wanting to see you covered in cum ever since you became legal."

"What?!!!" Remy's pussy leaked out even more cum after that unexpected reply.

Kiarra leaned against the door frame, undoing her hair so her raven locks flowed past her shoulders. She looked like she should be in a MILF shampoo commercial? Did they make MILF shampoo commercials? Did they make MILF shampoo? Remy would totally buy it if it gave her a better chance of fucking hot moms.

"Remy, you're the sexiest girl in the neighborhood," Kiarra continued. "Do you think I haven't fantasized about ravaging your young, co-ed body?"

Remy's jaw dropped. She couldn't believe the woman she had wet dreams about had also dreamt of fucking her. Would she have lost her virginity to Kiarra if she had known? The Italian sexpot could have surely taught a teenage Remy a lot about sex.

"You have excellent taste," Sam told Kiarra. "I love ravaging her slutty co-ed body too!"

"Are you a new friend?" Kiarra asked with her sexy accent.

"Yup! Well, a friend-boss. Remy's helping me with my science experiments over the summer."

"Oh, good," Kiarra replied, looking at Remy. "When I saw your parents the other day, they were hoping you could find a summer job."

Remy blushed. Knowing the woman was good friends with her parents made it more embarrassing that she was kneeling in front of her, naked and wet.

"Um, yeah," Remy replied, blushing. "I'm really enjoying working with Sam."

"And I'm really enjoying fucking her!" Sam said enthusiastically.

"Sam!" Remy blushed more. No one was attempting to

untie her or remove the dildos. It was mortifying sitting there with her holes stuffed, completely helpless while two older woman drank up her nude body. Mortifying but also hot as hell. Which is why Remy hadn't made any requests to be untied or freed of the delicious dildos.

"What?" Sam asked innocently. "You're not enjoying the fucking?"

"Oh my goodness, I love it!" Remy blurted, then blushed again, not intending to sound so desperate.

Kiarra smiled that gorgeous smile of hers. As a teen, that smile would make Remy run home and finger herself, dreaming about Kiarra taking her in her bedroom.

"I always knew you were a horny slut," she told Remy.

Remy gasped. "What? How did you know? Do I give off slut vibes?" She didn't realize everyone could tell what a whore she was just be looking at her. Oh no, did the whole neighborhood know she was a dirty slut? Would her parents lecture her about having safe sex with humans, aliens, and Bigfoots? And would all her neighbors proposition her the next time she saw them? That part didn't sound that bad actually. There were plenty of neighbors she wouldn't mind fucking.

"No, dear," Kiarra said with a laugh. "I watch you sunbathe in the nude in your backyard all the time. I figured you secretly desired to be naked and fucked as much as possible."

"Boy does she!" Sam exclaimed.

Remy ignored her kooky boss. She was too shocked by Kiarra's revelation. "How do you know I sunbathe naked?"

"Remember that high-powered telescope I have?"

"Uh huh." Kiarra knew Remy loved everything to do with space and had let the young woman gaze at the heavens many times. The view in their rural area was amazing. Remy loved talking with Kiarra about the stars. And loved being in the beautiful woman's presence. Even now at 40, Kiarra had lost none of her sex appeal. She had breasts that were the perfect size to fondle and a juicy ass that was unnaturally firm.

"I bring it up to my roof to spy on you when you're sunbathing," Kiarra confessed, though there was no shame behind that confession. In fact, she seemed rather proud of it.

Remy came again. All these bombshell revelations were giving her pussy a workout. "Oh my God, you've been watching me all those times I've been naked?"

"Of course. I know whenever your parents leave, you don't waste any time ripping your clothes off and running out to sunbathe. I particularly like it when you play with yourself."

Remy turned every shade of red in the spectrum. She thought no one knew about her naughty sunbathing and masturbation sessions. It turned out Kiarra had been secretly watching her this entire time, ogling her naughty college body.

"Holy shit!" Sam exclaimed. "You're even sluttier than I thought. Way to go, Remy!"

That made Remy feel a little better, but she was still beyond embarrassed.

Kiarra knelt beside her, running her gentle fingers along Remy's thigh. "How does that make you feel, knowing I was watching you?"

Remy's pussy kept spasming. Damn, Kiarra could make her cum just through sexy talk. She was so talented. Remy knew the woman must have a wealth of sensual knowledge to impart.

"Um, r… really embarrassed. B… but also really hot."

Kiarra's fingers moved higher. "You like being watched when you're naughty, don't you?"

Remy thought back to the aliens watching her get fucked, Sam watching T-69 pound her, and now Kiarra staring at her helpless, nude body. "I love it!"

"Wow, you're good!" Sam marveled, kneeling on the other side of Remy and touching her other thigh. "Wanna help me fuck this slut?"

Kiarra grinned. "Absolutely." She closed the dressing room door and began to strip, revealing sensual, tan skin.

Remy's eyes went wide. "Miss Costa, you're going to fuck me?"

"What did I say about the Miss Costa thing."

"I'm sorry!"

"Don't worry, I'll just have to spank you as punishment."

"Remy loves getting spanked!" Sam told her helpfully.

Kiarra grinned again. "Good. I love disciplining naughty college girls' asses."

Remy trembled. How many college girls had Kiarra fucked? Did she go around, seducing all the local co-eds, taking them back to her place, where she could have her way with her? What a woman! Remy wanted to become one of Kiarra's conquests.

"But to answer your question, dear," the Italian continued. "Yes, I'm going to fuck you. I've been waiting a long time to get my hands on your body."

Remy couldn't stop shaking. She couldn't believe she was about to have sex with the woman she had spent her teen years fantasizing about.

Sam patted Remy's leg. "Remy would love for you to fuck her."

"Sam! Can I answer for myself?"

"Oh c'mon, don't tell me you haven't been dreaming of fucking Kiarra since you were a horny youngster."

Remy blushed, nervous to admit it.

Kiarra squeezed Remy's leg, very close to her pussy. "Don't worry, dear, I always knew you had a crush on me."

"You did?"

"Sure. Why do you think I wore all those skimpy bikinis? I wanted to give you something to masturbate to."

"Oh my God, I fingered myself so many times after seeing you in one of those thongs."

Kiarra smiled. "Good. I like inspiring girls to pleasure themselves."

"Thank you for providing such amazing inspiration!" Remy replied. In a way, Kiarra had helped her get in touch with her sexual side. This was one wise woman.

"Wait a minute," Sam interrupted, also getting close to Remy's pussy. It was like she and Kiarra were competing to see whose fingers could get the closest without actually touching it. The teasing was driving Remy wild. "If you knew Remy had a crush on you, how come you never fucked her?"

"Well, I had to wait until she came of age. But even then, I was such good friends with her parents, I just... felt a little bad about wanting her."

"Don't feel bad," Remy blurted. "Please want me!"

Sam and Kiarra giggled.

"That's our slut," Sam chirped.

"She's quite desperate, isn't she?" Kiarra added.

"Of course I'm desperate!" Remy cried. "I'm tied up and have two huge sex toys in me, and the two most beautiful woman I've ever seen are naked and feeling me up." She squirmed around, showing exactly how desperate she was.

Kiarra patted the young woman's thigh. "Okay, we'll put you out of your misery. But we can't tell your parents."

"Oh my God, no, they can't know anything! Please don't tell them about this or all the ways Sam is fucking me for her sex experiments."

Kiarra gasped at Remy's revelation. "Your summer job is to be experimented on sexually?"

"Oops, did I not mention that?"

Sam rolled on the floor, laughing. "Man, you can't help but spill the beans about how slutty you are."

"I didn't mean to! It just came out."

"Oh it's going to come out," the pretty Asian replied. "Cum out of your pussy once we're done with you."

"I agree," Kiarra said, her eyes burning with lust. "Let's dominate this dirty slut."

They each grabbed one of the strap-ons from Sam's bag, eyeing Remy like she was their sex slave.

Remy shivered. She was about to be fucked by two beautiful, older women.

This might just be the best day of her life!

Chapter 13

Sam and Kiarra untied Remy and removed the vibrators from her pussy and ass. But her holes were only freed for a moment: the older women stood her up and shoved their strap-ons into her.

"Ohhh my God!!" Remy squealed, the pink and purple dildos sliding inside her dual tightness. Kiarra was handling her front while Sam took her rear.

They pushed all the way into her, sandwiching her between their lovely nude bodies. They left Remy fully impaled, making sure she realized she was their slut.

Remy trembled against the beautiful female flesh surrounding her. She wanted to be their slut. She wanted to obey their every command.

She closed her eyes, feeling their breasts against her chest and back, their hands roaming her young body.

"You like being double penetrated, don't you, dear?" Kiarra asked, rubbing Remy's cheek.

"Y… yes," Remy replied breathlessly.

Sam spanked her. "Yup, this slut's never happy unless she has two big cocks inside her." To prove her point, she shoved her anal dildo farther up Remy's back door.

"Uhhhhhhh!" the college girl moaned. "Fuck, Sam, that's deep!"

"What's that, you want it deeper? You got it!" The mischievous scientist shoved the toy as far as she could up Remy's ass.

Remy tensed and clasped Kiarra tightly. "Oh fuck, I'm such a butt slut!"

The Italian beauty smiled. "I'm glad to hear it, honey. I agree with Sam, you should always have your pussy and ass probed."

Remy nodded. "Y… yes, of course. I'll do whatever you two think is best for my pussy and ass."

Sam giggled. "Wow, you've become so much sluttier than when we first met. I'm impressed!"

"Um, thanks?" Remy wasn't sure if that was good or bad. Up until a few days ago, she never would have imagined she'd be having all this kinky, submissive sex. Or that she would have been ravaged by aliens, robots, and cryptids. A whole new world of sexuality had opened up before her. And she loved it!

Kiarra stroked Remy's hair. "I'm impressed too. I should have been dominating you much sooner."

"You can dominate me anytime you want!" Remy confessed. "You too, Sam."

"Wonderful, honey," Kiarra replied. "From now on,

whenever you come over to my house, I expect you to strip and become my sex slave."

"Yes, ma'am!" Remy answered before even thinking about it. She'd been dreaming about being the MILF's sex slave for years.

Sam fondled Remy's ass. "And don't worry, I already know I can dominate you whenever I want. I still have lots of sexy inventions to test out on you. I'll have you cumming all the time!"

Remy almost came just hearing that. Besides all the sci-fi creatures who had been owning her slutty body, she now had two hot, older women who were claiming her as their own. Remy was going to be spending the whole summer getting fucked. Best summer ever!

"Okay, enough talking," Sam decided. "Let's fuck this slut!"

Kiarra liked that idea, and the two thrust in and out of Remy with their fake cocks.

Remy flung her arms around Kiarra's neck and hung on for dear life as she was double fucked. Kiarra soothed her with sensual descriptions of how beautiful the young woman's pussy was while Sam made cruder remarks about how she loved ramming Remy's tight ass.

As far as Remy was concerned, they could say whatever they wanted as long as they kept pounding her. They were in perfect sync, the dildos filling her pussy and ass at the same time. When they did, Remy felt like she might explode. But instead she just had an explosive orgasm. She screamed into Kiarra's shoulder and splattered her juices across her childhood crush's thighs.

"Nice!" Sam commented. "Let's fuck her harder and give her a bunch of orgasms in a row."

"Excellent idea," Kiarra agreed.

They slammed Remy's holes like they were drilling for oil and gave her one climax after another.

"I… can't… stop… cumming!!!" she said between orgasmic moans.

Sam squeezed Remy's butt. "Great! You shouldn't stop."

Kiarra squeezed Remy's breasts. "You'll never stop when you're with us."

"O… okay." Remy couldn't refuse either of the gorgeous women. They were her seniors, so she obviously had to do whatever they said. And if they commanded her to constantly cum, that's what she would do. Wow, she was getting really good at being submissive. Who knew she was such a natural at it?

The Italian and Asian beauties finally stopped once Remy had made a big mess of herself and the floor.

Sam hugged her from behind. "Remy, you're the best! You're an amazing slut!"

"Th… thanks," the amazing slut replied, barely able to stand. These were weird compliments, but Remy didn't mind. Sam was a weird, kinky girl.

"I agree," Kiarra added. "I'm so proud of you, honey." She brushed Remy's sweaty locks out of her face.

Remy beamed. She didn't realize how much the older woman's approval meant to her. But she was very happy to live up to Kiarra's slut standards.

The Italian hottie glanced over Remy's shoulder. "But I think you also enjoy being a slut," she said to Sam.

"Me?" the Asian cutie replied.

"Oh yeah," Remy said. "Sam's just as big of a slut as me. She loves going outside and begging handymen to rail her."

"Hey! That was just the one time. And you got railed too."

"Well, yeah, he had a really nice set of tools." Remy giggled along with Sam, fondly remembering their time tied to her jeep while the hunky Mr. Fix-It had his way with them.

"All right, enough giggling, girls. On your knees." Kiarra's tone brooked no disagreement, so Remy and Sam knelt before their Italian mistress. Of course, first Sam had to take her dildo out of Remy's butt, and Kiarra had to remove hers from Remy's sopping wet pussy.

The boutique manager swiped Sam's strap-on but kept hers on. She moved the purple monster to the sexy scientist's lips. It was dripping with Remy's juices.

"Clean off your new assistant's cum," Kiarra ordered.

Sam's eyes lit up. "Yum!" She immediately went to work, licking the tip before deep-throating the fake cock.

Remy stared wide-eyed at her friend. She had no idea Sam was that eager to taste her juices. What a great boss!

"Remy, honey, scoot next to Sam so your bare legs are touching," Kiarra commanded in a sweet but firm manner.

"Yes, Kiarra." Remy scooted. She loved touching Sam's skin and tingled as soon as their legs made contact.

Kiarra ran her fingers through her two sluts' hair, watching Sam suck off the dildo. "Do you like watching Sam lick your juices?" she asked Remy.

"Ohhhh yeah." Remy couldn't take her eyes off the Asian beauty. Sam gave great blowjobs. Though she was even better at eating tight pussies.

"Good. But now it's your turn." Kiarra yanked Sam's head off the dildo and presented it to Remy.

"Hey, I wasn't done!" Sam complained.

"Don't worry, you'll have a chance to perform a lot more oral soon," Kiarra reassured her.

"Oh, good!" That made the sex scientist happy, so she contented herself with watching Remy.

The college girl eyed the huge dildo. Sam had done a good job cleaning it, but there was still plenty of fluid on it. Remy had really drenched it.

"You want me to lick off my own juices?" she asked Kiarra.

"Of course, dear. Aren't you used to doing that?"

"Yup! Well, ever since I met Sam."

"Woohoo!" the sneaky scientist cheered. "I'm such a good influence."

Kiarra patted her head. "You certainly are. Let's see how well you've taught our young slut. Get to work, Remy."

"Yes, ma'am." Remy loved obeying Kiarra. She felt naturally submissive to the beautiful, older woman. She wanted to please her, wanted to serve her every sexual desire.

She licked up and down the sides of the dildo, tasting herself and feeling very naughty. Then she circled the tip before taking it in her mouth.

Kiarra snatched Remy's hair and forced the pretend cock into the young woman's throat. "Be a good girl and take the whole thing."

Remy wanted to be a good girl, so she deep throated it, nearly gagging. She got used to it after a few thrusts and enjoyed tasting herself as Kiarra thrust in and out of her slutty mouth.

"Fuck, that's so hot!" Sam exclaimed. Her right hand had traveled between her legs and was currently rubbing her cute, tight slit.

Kiarra thrust in one last time, leaving it fully in Remy's throat for a few seconds before finally pulling out.

Remy gasped, sucking in oxygen and dripping her cum

from her lips.

Kiarra knelt in front of her and kissed her. It was soft and sweet, and she did things with her tongue Remy had never experienced before. She really needed to get with older women more often. They were excellent teachers.

"You did such a good job, honey," Kiarra told her. "I love seeing your cum all over your face."

"Me too!!" Sam squealed as she squirted across her thighs.

Kiarra kept her hands on Remy, letting them roam gently across the submissive co-ed's body. "Your friend is quite naughty," she said. "I don't remember telling her to play with herself."

"Sam is super-naughty," Remy agreed. "She's always getting me into embarrassing sexual situations."

"Ohhhh!" Sam came again. "Hey, that's only happened like, um, every time we've hung out."

Kiarra smiled. "I can't wait to hear about all these sexy embarrassing situations. But first, I want both you girls to eat me out." She stood, presenting her bush to them.

Remy and Sam beamed and clasped Kiarra's thighs, Remy taking the right and Sam the left. They tag-teamed her pussy, running their tongues up and down the gorgeous Italian's slit.

Kiarra had a trim bush, and Remy enjoyed exploring the small forest to get to the treasure of her neighbor's juicy lips.

When she penetrated those lips, Remy sighed, knowing her fifteen year-old self was finally getting her dreams to come true.

"Hey, don't hog her pussy," Sam scolded, forcing her tongue in next to Remy's. The two jockeyed for position, determined to be the one who pleased their mistress the most.

Kiarra grabbed their hair and yanked their heads back. "Girls, don't fight. Work together to make me cum all over your faces."

"Yes, ma'am!" the girls replied before diving back in.

Remy's tongue touched Sam's within Kiarra's warm womb. It was like she was kissing the naughty scientist while pleasuring Kiarra's pussy. It was true bliss.

"Mmm," Kiarra cooed. "Just like that, girls.

That inspired them to go harder, and they explored every nook and cranny in the 40-year-old pussy.

When Remy felt Kiarra was getting close to climax, she switched to her clit, letting Sam stay inside Kiarra's warm lips. The Italian's clit was large and throbbed and begged Remy to touch it.

She did, licking it lightly to tease the older woman before wrapping her lips around it and sucking.

"Ohhhhhh God!!!" Kiarra wailed before exploding all over Remy and Sam's faces.

They weren't prepared for how powerful a squirter their

new mistress was. They yelped in surprise as they were blasted with cum shots. But being professional sluts, they took it like champs and eagerly lapped up the Italian juices.

Remy loved how the older woman tasted. She hoped she could eat her out every day. Hmm, she was going to have to make a schedule: she had to work for Sam, set aside extra time to fuck Sam, go to Kiarra's house to be a sex slave, visit Bigfoot for more furry fun, and be a sex ambassador for aliens. This was turning into one busy summer.

Kiarra kissed both of them and then commanded them to kiss each other.

Remy and Sam happily complied, French kissing like horny teens. Well, actually Remy was only one year beyond being a horny teen. She had spent a bunch of her teen years thinking about sex and masturbating, though she didn't actually have that much sex. She supposed she was making up for it now.

There was a knock on the dressing room door, and it opened, revealing a Bouncy Boutique employee. She was in her mid-20s and very cute.

"Oh, sorry," she said. "I didn't realize you were fucking sluts in here."

Remy gasped. What the heck? Was this a common occurrence in Kiarra's store? Did she often take customers into the dressing room and fuck the shit out of them? No wonder this store was so popular.

"Um, hello," Remy said awkwardly to the employee.

"Hi!" Sam greeted the woman. "We're definitely big sluts!"

Remy rolled her eyes. She didn't know if Sam needed to confirm that. Of course, the fact that they were naked, kneeling in front of Kiarra, and covered in cum was probably a good giveaway.

"Hey!" the employee replied. "Nice to meet you!" She seemed to have no problem meeting wet, naked girls. Remy liked this lady. "Kiarra, I need your help with a customer."

"Of course," the store manager replied. "Just help me tie these two up first."

"We're getting tied up?" Remy asked.

"Remy, honey, don't be silly. When you're tied up, I can have a lot more fun with you." Kiarra smiled and stroked her young slut's hair.

"Oh, right. Please tie us up!" Remy presented her hands, eager to be bound by her childhood crush.

Sam did the same. The scientist never turned down an opportunity to be bound and fucked.

Kiarra tied Remy's hands behind her back with soft silk while her cute employee took care of Sam.

"Serena, can you grab the double dildo?" Kiarra asked her colleague once the sluts were bound.

"Sure thing!" the woman scooted out and was back in a flash with a big, curved sex toy.

Remy eyed the dildo, surprised Serena was able to get it so fast. Did Kiarra keep a stock of sex toys in the dressing room area? Well, that would make sense if she was always fucking girls while they tried on clothes.

Kiarra and Serena positioned the double dildo between Remy and Sam, instructing them to ease their pussies onto it.

They did, moaning in tandem as their holes were filled. Remy's knees straddled Sam's, their bodies close as they worked to take more of the dildo.

"That's great," Kiarra told them. "I'll be back in a bit. In the meantime, feel free to cum as much as you want."

"Ohhhh," Remy moaned. "O… okay. Thank you!"

Sam moaned her thanks as well, her cute pussy trembling around the big cock.

Kiarra and Serena closed the door behind them, leaving Remy and Sam tied up, convulsing on the delicious sex toy.

Remy sighed. She couldn't go anywhere nowadays without getting bound and fucked.

It was so great!

Chapter 14

Remy wiggled on the double dildo, loving how it felt inside her tightness.

Sam did the same on the other end, her cute tits bouncing around. "This is fun!"

Remy nodded. It was fun being tied up with Sam, forced to fuck a huge sex toy. "Kiarra's really good at domination."

"Oh yeah! You have one kinky neighbor. I bet she's going to come to your house all the time and turn you into her sex slave."

"You really think so?"

"Yup. She's a woman who takes what she wants."

"She can take me!" Remy exclaimed. "But what if my parents are home when she wants to dominate me?"

"She can fuck you in your bedroom. But you better not scream too loud." Sam smirked, knowing that would be impossible for her young assistant.

"Sam! You know I'm a huge, slutty screamer."

"Oh yeah, you're the best I've ever heard. I go to sleep each night to an audio loop of your sluttiest moans."

Remy gasped, both from that tidbit and from the dildo

sliding farther inside her. “What?! You have more recordings of me?”

“Just the ones from T-69 fucking you. I made a mix tape.” The naughty scientist smiled, very proud of herself.

“Ack!” Remy yelped. “That's so embarrassing!”

“That's so hot, you mean.”

Remy sighed. “Well, at least you don't have the recordings the aliens took of me.”

“Alien sex recordings?!!!” Sam cried, so shocked she accidentally impaled herself on the dildo and squirted across Remy's tits.

Sam panted with her tongue hanging out, recovering from her surprise orgasm. “Oh boy, that was good. But… aliens?!!!”

Remy blushed. “Oh, um, yeah, remember I mentioned I had met extraterrestrials.”

“Yeah, but I got so busy fucking you I totally forgot. I'm a terrible geeky scientist!”

“You're a super-sexy geeky scientist!” Remy screamed as she had her own orgasm and soaked Sam's thighs.

“Thank you! And thanks for the cum bath. You're an adorable assistant.”

Remy giggled. Only a goofball like Sam would enjoy being cum on so much. Oh wait, Remy loved being cum on too. Guess she was a sexy goofball as well. She was cool with that. Her friends already thought she was weird for her love of cheesy sci-fi movies. They probably would think fucking aliens, robots, and cryptids was weird too. But that's just because they hadn't tried it. What girl could turn down a sci-fi dick?

"Now tell me everything about the aliens!" Sam demanded while continuing to fuck her cute cunt. Sam had a very tight pussy and large objects made her utter sweet erotic noises. Remy was a big fan of those noises.

"Well, the day before I met you, I was on my way back from a sci-fi movie marathon and a group of gray aliens abducted me."

"Holy shit! Wait, gray? So they look like all those drawings?"

"Yup."

"Did they experiment on you?"

"Oh yeah. They probed my pussy, ass, mouth. And then, um, they made me pleasure all five of them at once."

"You lucky slut!"

Remy nodded. "It was amazing. I couldn't stop myself from wanting their big alien cocks. Plus, I wanted to be polite and give them a good impression of Earth."

Sam laughed so hard she made herself have another orgasm. "Ohhhhhahahaha!" she scream-giggled.

"Hey! What's so funny?"

"I love how your politeness makes you spread your legs for aliens."

"But I like being polite."

Sam smiled. "I'm just teasing. Why do you think I've got it so bad for you? You're such a sweet and super-friendly girl."

Remy's cheeks turned the color of her pussy lips. "Oh, thanks Sam! But I thought you liked me for my tits and ass."

"Oh, I love those! But I like hanging out with you because you're an adorable nerd."

"I love being an adorable nerd!" Remy cheered, then climaxed. Talking about being a nerd while on a dildo usually did that to her.

"So what else did you let the aliens do to you to make sure they knew Earth girls are all sluts?"

"I don't think all Earth girls are sluts," Remy replied.

"But you sure are."

"Hey, so are you!"

"Oh yeah, I'm a big slut." Sam rammed her pussy on the dildo again and sprayed Remy's stomach. She seemed intent on covering her younger friend in as much cum as possible.

Remy giggled. "Okay, you silly slut, I'll tell you what else they did."

"Yes!"

"When they abducted me the second time, they had a beautiful, blue alien girl with them. And she had tentacles for hair."

"Holy hentai!" Sam cried. "Please tell me she fucked you

with her tentacles."

"Hell yeah! She was super-skilled with them. But she was really sweet too. And then we let the aliens treat us both like fuck toys."

Sam kept cumming during Remy's tale. "This is the greatest story in history! I'm so jealous! Can you please convince them to abduct me with you?"

"Well, the last time I was on their ship they made me the official Sex Ambassador for Earth. So I'm sure they'd be fine if I bring another Earth girl with me."

"I want to be that Earth girl!" Sam begged. "Please, please, please!"

"Hmm," Remy replied. "I'm not sure if you're slutty enough for the aliens."

"What?!" Sam said in shock. "I'm super-slutty. I'm the sluttiest scientist who's ever lived!"

Remy smiled. "Okay, you can come."

"Yay! Hey, wait, were you teasing me?"

"Yup. I need to get you back for all your sneaky teasing."

"I guess that's fair," Sam agreed amiably. "When do I get to meet the aliens?"

As if summoning them from the heavens, a beam of white light engulfed the naked girls, and they vanished.

They rematerialized on the alien ship, still tied up and still impaled by the double dildo.

The five gray aliens gazed upon Remy with their

unblinking eyes.

"Oh, hi guys!" she greeted them warmly. "We were just talking about you. This is my friend, Sam. Can she be an alien slut with me?"

Sam's mouth hung open, staring in shock at the short-statured creatures.

"Um, Sam, are you okay?" Remy asked.

"A… a… aliens!!!" the nude scientist shrieked.

"Yup, these are the aliens I told you about." Remy didn't know what the big deal was. She was used to getting beamed up by her extraterrestrial friends. But, of course, this was Sam's first alien experience, so her shock was understandable.

The Asian beauty trembled. "I can't believe they're real."

"I told you they were real. As a true geek girl, I would never make something like that up."

"I know, I'm sorry. I wasn't doubting your nerd credentials. It's just… seeing them in person, I… I can't describe it."

Remy nodded. She had a similar reaction the first time they abducted her. "Wait until they fuck you."

Sam trembled even more. "Yes, please!"

The grays pointed to the large dildo.

"Oh, that," Remy said. "We were kind of in the middle of getting tied up and fucked by my MILF-y neighbor."

"Do they know what a MILF is?" Sam asked.

"Oops, good point. A MILF is a really hot… wait a minute, you guys can't understand anything I'm saying. Why am I telling you this?"

Sam gasped. "They don't have a universal translator."

Remy shook her head. "Nope. Not everything's like Star Trek."

"Rats."

Remy nodded empathetically. She had often fantasized about serving in Starfleet. Of course, she was having her own real-life galactic encounter right now. And it involved super-kinky sex. So it was even better than Star Trek! "Last time, the tentacle girl translated for me," she told Sam.

Right on cue, Kigami appeared before them as a shimmering, blue hologram.

"Hello, my beautiful human friend," she said.

"Kigami!" Remy exclaimed. "I'm so happy to see you. But why aren't you here in person?"

"I was required to return to my home planet to participate in our annual, planet-wide orgy."

Remy and Sam trembled so much on the dildo they made themselves cum.

"As free with your fluids as ever, I see," Kigami commented.

Remy moaned. "Uh… uh huh. Your planet is amazing!"

"I like it," the holo-girl replied. "I see you have a sexy friend with you."

"Oh, yeah. This is Sam. I'm working for her over the summer as her sci-fi sex toy."

"Ooh, I love that name," Sam said. "Your official job title is now Sci-Fi Sex Toy."

"Okay! Wait, is that what I have to put on my resume?"

"Yup. It will open a lot of doors for you."

"Um, I think it will just lead to me opening my legs a lot."

"That's good too!"

Kigami smiled. "Your friend is as horny as you."

Remy nodded. "She sure is! She's begging to be fucked by aliens."

"That is fortuitous for it is why the grays have summoned you. They have brought another species with them and wish you to officially welcome them as the Sex Ambassador for Earth."

"Yes!" Remy cheered. "My first official duty as sex ambassador." She didn't realize she'd be so excited about it, but after getting a taste of alien cum, it was hard not to want more, especially a new variety. She wondered what these other aliens looked like.

"Can I be the sex ambassador's assistant?" Sam asked.

The grays looked at Kigami, communicating with her telepathically. Remy was fascinated to see the telepathic link worked over holo-communication. Alien technology was cool!

Kigami turned to Sam. "They said they expect you to be just as much of a whore as Remy."

"Hey!" Remy protested.

"It's a term of endearment," Kigami explained. "You did let them fuck you however they wanted last time. And took every single one of their cocks."

Remy licked her lips, remembering the fun experience. "Well, that's true. Okay, I'm their whore!"

"I'll be their whore too!" Sam volunteered.

Kigami smiled. "Excellent. They were monitoring your activities in that closet down on Earth. You both were acting like very big sluts."

"Closet?" Remy asked in confusion. "Oh, you mean the dressing room. Yeah, Kiarra fucked us so good. Wait, they were watching that?"

"Of course," Kigami replied. "They can spy on you anytime they want."

"Ack! That means they've seen me do all sorts of naughty stuff."

Kigami giggled. "My sweet human girl, you've done all sorts of naughty stuff on their ship."

Sam joined the giggling. "She's got you there."

"Okay, I suppose that makes sense," Remy admitted. "But it's kinda embarrassing knowing they can look at me naked and watch me have sex whenever they want."

"They are quite voyeuristic," Kigami agreed.

Sam hopped up and down. "I really like these aliens!" The hopping, of course, made her have another orgasm.

"It appears you two are ready to be fucked," Kigami noted. "I must return to my planet's orgy, but the grays will take good care of you."

Remy shivered. By taking good care of them, she knew Kigami meant the grays and their alien buddies were going to fuck the shit out of her and Sam. Thank goodness!

"Okay, thanks, Kigami," she told the blue beauty. "I can't with to have sex with you again."

"Do not worry, my human slut. I'll return soon and shove my tendrils in all your tightest spots." She grinned and then blipped out.

"Alien girls are so cool!" Sam marveled.

"Uh huh," Remy agreed. "I need her tentacles!"

"Damn, these aliens have really made you horny. No wonder you've become an even bigger slut."

Remy nodded. "Well, it's certainly helped. Though you and T-69 have been a huge part of my slut training too."

"Yay! I love training sluts."

Remy chuckled. This was one kooky scientist she had as a friend.

"Okay, we're ready to be fucked!" she told her gray buddies.

One of the aliens interacted with a holo-screen, and a circular section of the floor opened.

A platform raised from a lower area of the ship.

Remy watched it eagerly. She didn't know the ship had a lower deck.

Four members of a very different alien species rose into view. They had green, scaly skin, thick tails, and long tongues. They looked like huge lizard men. And they had huge lizard dicks.

Remy gasped. Oh fuck, what had she signed up for?

Chapter 15

The lizard men's tongues snaked out in anticipation upon seeing the naked human girls.

They snatched Remy and Sam off the double dildo, two holding the college co-ed and two the sexy scientist.

"Oh shit!" Sam wailed. "I've never been fucked by aliens before." She wiggled nervously in the lizards' powerful claws.

"Sam, it'll be okay, I promise," Remy soothed her. "Aliens are really good at fucking human girls."

Sam took a couple of deep breaths. "Right. You're the expert. Sorry I freaked out. I've been fantasizing about being fucked by aliens forever, but I'm nervous now that it's actually happening."

Remy was close enough to take her friend's hand. She understood the trepidation that came with a girl's first alien fucking. "I'll be with you the whole time. It'll be fun to get fucked together."

"Yes! I love getting fucked with you." That made Sam relax. She and Remy had been fucked together multiple times already, each time furthering their slutty bond of friendship.

The two lizard men manhandling Remy fought over who would be the first to fuck her.

"Ack!" she yelped. "C'mon, boys, can't you take turns? I promise I'll fuck every one of you. It's my official duty as sex ambassador." Remy always took jobs seriously, not that she had ever been a sex ambassador before. But that was why she had to do her absolute best.

"You're an inspiration to sluts everywhere!" Sam told her as the other two lizards fought over her. Remy was glad to see that so many alien species desired human females. Maybe Earth girls would become the most desired sluts in the galaxy!

The lizards decided to compromise and spit-roasted Remy. They held her in the air between them, one shoving his dick in her mouth, the other her pussy.

The cocks were scaly and felt weird. But the scales just stimulated her pussy more than usual. And her mouth got used to them after a few thrusts.

The lizard men were strong, easily holding her aloft as they rammed her. She felt helpless and submissive, exactly how she liked it when she had sex with aliens.

Sam was getting a similar spit-roasting, the other two lizards inspired by their brethren. The cute scientist whimpered and moaned amid her sucking sounds.

The grays stood nearby, nodding to each other as they

took mental notes. Remy wondered if they were recording her again. As long as it was for research purposes, she didn't mind. It seemed like everyone was making videos of her sexcapades lately. She kept trying to resist the idea of becoming an alien porn star. Did aliens like lesbian porn? Maybe Sam could join her. Ahh, she needed to stop thinking such dirty stuff. And go back to being fucked like a dirty slut!

Which is exactly what the lizards did. Their cocks were so large they easily dominated her pussy and mouth. They spoke in a harsh, guttural language. Remy didn't know what they were saying, but she was pretty sure they were commenting on how human girls were huge whores.

The two sluts continued to be fucked, the lizards having impressive stamina. Just when Remy was wondering when they were going to cum, they unleashed their lizard seed inside her. It was strong and thick and coated her throat and the walls of her pussy.

They dropped her to the floor and stroked their cocks, cumming across her naked body.

Sam plopped next to her and got the same treatment from her alien lovers. The scientist looked very happy, sighing as glops of cum splattered her cute curves. "Ohh wow, aliens can really fuck."

"Uh huh," Remy agreed. She was glad she had a friend to share alien fucking with.

The lizards gave the girls no time to rest. The two who had speared Remy plucked her off the ground and held her in the air, both of their tongues penetrating her pussy.

"Holy fuck!!" she screamed. She had never experienced tongues like theirs: they were long, forked, and agile. They were able to reach all the way to her cervix and do tricks inside her womb like she had never felt before.

The one lizard attacked her from the front, the other from behind. That one's tongue brushed her ass as it penetrated her pussy. The two tongues filled her pleasantly as they fucked her.

She cried and moaned, deciding that lizards were made to eat out girls' cooches.

Sam was getting a dual tongue fucking as well and competed with Remy for who could scream the loudest.

One of the scaly suckers latched on to Remy's clit with its forked tongue and tugged. She let out an orgasmic scream that reverberated around the ship, her cum flowing out of her like she had been hoarding it for years.

The two lizard men fought to lap it up, acting like it was the nectar of the gods. Remy was starting to really like these reptiles.

Sam squealed and opened her floodgates, making the other two lizards quite happy.

The two aliens controlling Remy's body tossed her to their friends, exchanging her for Sam.

Remy's new lizard mates held her upside down, plunging their tongues inside her cunt.

Sam got the same treatment from Remy's first lizard lovers, dangling beside the naked co-ed. "Ohhhh fuck, I bet my pussy is tastier to them than yours."

"No way!" Remy retorted. "Sex ambassadors always have the tastiest pussies."

Sam giggled. "So that's how you got the job."

"Yup!" Actually, she got it because she was the first slut the aliens had fucked on Earth. But Kigami had told her the grays thought she was perfect for the role, which was a nice compliment.

"Well, they're doing a taste test, so I guess we'll find out," Sam squealed.

"I like these kind of tests," Remy said, squirming upside down as the lizards made her spill her fluids again. She wondered if the lizard men went around space, tasting different female pussies to see which was the most delectable. That would be a noble pursuit.

The girls' juices ran from their cunts to their stomachs and across their tits until reaching their lips. They dutifully drank their cum, knowing alien males really liked that. Or at least Remy assumed they did. The grays had never complained when she tasted her own essence. Of course, they never said anything since they communicated telepathically. But as sex ambassador, she had learned what they liked and how best to please them.

"Fu... fuck!" Sam whimpered. "They won't stop eating our pussies."

"Y... yeah!" Remy wailed. "I love aliens!"

"Me too!"

Remy smiled through her moaning. She was glad Sam had taken to being an alien fuck toy so quickly. Remy would have felt weird if she was the only girl who loved getting railed by sexy aliens.

The lizards might not have been sexy, but they had big dicks and long tongues and loved eating pussies, so they were all right in Remy's book.

After giving the girls a million orgasms, they dropped them to the floor again.

"Oof," Remy groaned. These lizards were good at fucking but could be a little gentler handling human bodies.

She clutched Sam, the two sluts trembling as post-orgasmic pulses shot through them.

The four lizard men lay side by side on the floor, their huge reptilian dicks standing straight up.

The grays pointed to Remy and Sam and then to the lizard penises.

"Oh, you want us to fuck all four of their big dicks?" Remy said. "Okay!"

"How do you know that's what they meant?" Sam asked.

"Well, they always want me to fuck something, so it's a

pretty safe bet. They seem to think human girls only exist to be fucked."

Sam giggled, elbowing Remy. "I wonder how they got that idea."

"Hey! Just because I fuck them every time I come onboard and let them treat me like a slut, that..." Remy stopped, realizing how it sounded. "Oh, okay, I guess that's how they got that idea."

Sam patted her friend's tush. "Don't be embarrassed. You've done a great thing for man, er, womankind. Who doesn't want to be an alien slut?"

"Right!" Remy cheered. Okay, so probably not everyone wanted to be an alien slut, but all the cool girls did. What cool girls were those? Remy wasn't sure, but Sam was one of them. She bet Kiarra would enjoy watching her and Sam get dominated by aliens. And her best friend Lily might not mind an alien fucking either. She hadn't done anything too kinky that Remy knew about, but there might be an epic slut just waiting to burst out of that cute body. That's what happened to Remy. She had no idea how much she wanted to be dominated by sexy creatures until the gray aliens abducted her and did all those nifty experiments.

So it was her duty to reinforce the aliens' idea that all human women were big sluts. She jumped on the first green cock, letting it sink deep within her womb. "Ohhhhh God, it's so big!" She rode the lizard cowgirl style while giving his friend a handjob.

Sam did her own cowgirl tricks on the lizard on the other end and provided her own handy to his buddy.

When the girls got their cunts filled with cum, they switched to the neighboring scaly dick and rode that. They made sure to take all four cocks, getting filled with four different flavors of reptile cum.

When they were done, they sat against the wall of the alien ship, panting.

"I'm so sticky," Remy said, indicating both her body and her pussy.

"Yeah, lizard cum is really thick," Sam agreed. "I better make an invention to flush it all out of us."

"I love your inventions."

"Aha! So you do love it when T-69 dominates you."

Remy blushed. "Of course. It's just embarrassing when he fucks me in front of people and makes me say so many slutty things."

"I love it when he does that," Sam replied with a grin. "But, wait, you aren't embarrassed to fuck aliens?"

"Nope."

"How come?"

Remy considered it. She had some trepidation when they first fucked her, but she had quickly taken to the grays' desire to sexually experiment on her. "I'm not sure. It just seems right that aliens should fuck human girls."

Sam giggled. "You're a true sci-fi slut!"

"Thank you!" Remy was happy with that title. She was becoming a big fan of fucking aliens.

And the aliens were apparently a big fan of fucking her and Sam. The lizards spoke in their guttural tongue to the grays, who nodded and picked the girls up from the floor.

Remy let them guide her to the rear of the ship, where they had first experimented on her. She also let heir hands roam her body. They had let the lizard men have all the fun, so it was only right they get to cop a feel.

Sam yelped cutely as her butt was grabbed. Remy enjoyed seeing her friend groped by aliens. And Sam definitely enjoyed being groped.

The grays led them to two pods that were placed against the far wall.

"What are these?" Remy asked.

The nearest gray replied by whacking Remy on the ass, propelling her toward the pod.

"Ack! Okay, okay, I'm going." These aliens really liked her butt. They were cool that way.

Sam got her own booty propelled forward, and both girls clambered in to the standing pods, turning around to face the grays and lizards.

Metal restrains encircled their arms, legs, and hips.

"Yikes!" Sam yelped. "What's going on?"

"Um, I'm not sure," Remy replied as her legs were

spread by the restraints. "It's probably another one of their kinky experiments."

"Oh, okay. I like kinky experiments. Especially when I'm doing them on you."

Remy rolled her eyes. She knew full well how much Sam loved using her inventions to turn Remy into a submissive slut.

A clear, plastic-looking cylinder rose from the bottom of the pod until it reached Remy's pussy. It fused to her lips with suction devices, creating an airtight seal.

A large dildo rose from inside the plastic cylinder, greeting Remy's lips with a powerful penetration.

"Ohhhh, that feels good!" she moaned.

"Fuck, yes!" Sam agreed, getting her own pussy penetration in the pod next to Remy.

The dildo thrust in and out of Remy's cunt, fucking her until she began leaking her juices. They went straight down into the cylinder, collecting at the bottom.

The robotic cocks fucked Remy and Sam faster and harder, making more of their juices pool up in the cum collectors attached to them.

The lizards licked their lips, staring at the increasing levels of girl cum.

Remy's eyes went wide. Oh fuck, the grays were pumping them for their cum so the lizards could take it with them.

Remy and Sam had become human juice machines!

Chapter 16

The dildo jackhammered Remy, plumbing her for all her tasty cum.

"Ohhhh fuuucckkkkk!" she wailed.

Sam thrashed back and forth in the pod next to her. "I can't stop leaking!" the cute Asian woman cried. A steady drip flowed from her tiny pussy.

"S… sorry, Sam," Remy said. "I… ohhh my God that's deep… didn't know they were going to do this."

"Don't apologize. It's awesome! We're being pussy milked by aliens!"

Remy gasped as the dildo went all the way inside her again. She was glad Sam was enjoying her alien abduction. And her sorta girlfriend/sorta boss was right: it was awesome! "Y… yeah, I guess they think we're really tasty."

"Hell yeah, we are! We've got the tastiest pussies on Earth!"

Remy giggled. She wasn't sure how Sam had made that assessment, but she was a sex scientist so probably had data on stuff like that. Remy wasn't going to complain about Sam and the aliens thinking she had a yummy cooch.

The robotic penises increased to an even higher intensity, which made Remy and Sam really open their floodgates.

Remy's entire body was a trembling mess. "Ohhhh my God!! It… it's fucking me so hard!"

"It's destroying my pussy!" Sam agreed, spraying her juicy cum all around the gigantic dildo.

The lizard men loved how the girls were flailing and squirting, so they stroked their scaly cocks and shot their hot seed across Remy and Sam's bodies.

"Fuck, lizards can really cum far!" Remy remarked.

"And they have excellent aim," Sam added, getting two sticky shots to her tits.

"They sure… ack!" Remy got a mouthful of lizard semen in the middle of her reply. She swallowed it like all good sex ambassadors knew how to do.

The grays apparently thought the lizards had the right idea. They joined in, playing with their big gray cocks until a mixture of alien cum was splattering the girls left and right.

With nine male aliens all spewing their seed, Remy and Sam were quickly coated in warm, gooey gunk.

"You guys are really making us feel like sluts," Remy remarked.

"I love being an alien slut!" Sam cheered.

"I told you it was great." Remy beamed, happy she had shown Sam the wonders of being an intergalactic whore.

Being covered in cum just made the two sluts cum even

more. They both filled their cylindrical containers with their girl juices. At which point, the grays removed the cylinders and replaced them with fresh ones.

"We… we're not done?" Remy asked.

"They really want a lot of our cum," Sam marveled.

A small device emerged from the pod and covered Remy's clit, fitting snugly around it.

"Ooh, that feels niicceeeeeeeeeeeee!!" The clit device activated, stimulating Remy's nub so hard her cum poured out of her like a fire hose.

"Aiieeeeeeeeeeeeee!!" Sam screamed, getting her own clit treatment.

Both girls pussies looked like faucets turned on full. They filled the new containers in less than a minute. The grays dutifully replaced them with new ones, which Remy and Sam filled as well.

This continued, with the girls filling container after container with their sweet human fluids.

Remy couldn't stop cumming. The clit vibration device had her in a state of never-ending climax. She lost track of how many containers she had filled. She wasn't even sure if she stayed conscious the whole time. Her brain was overloaded with the most extreme pleasure sensations she had ever felt.

But she knew she and Sam had become human cum machines, there to provide the lizards with as much of their nectar as the aliens desired.

She also knew she should probably be embarrassed to be turned into a pussy milk provider, and part of her was, but the other part of her loved being at the mercy of the aliens, loved being forced to have continuous, unbelievably intense orgasms. And it made sense that the Sex Ambassador for Earth would have to give parting gifts to visiting aliens. She just didn't know that gift would be gallons upon gallons of her cum.

She eventually did pass out. The last sounds she heard were Sam's cute, orgasmic screams.

***

She woke up against Sam's warm, nude body, which was absolutely the best way to wake up.

She was draped over Sam, who was on her back, snoozing away. Remy snuggled in closer, wanting to feel every inch of the sweet scientist. She had become very fond of the older woman and wanted to spend as much time as possible in her naked embrace.

But then she realized something: they were no longer on the alien ship. They were… in her bedroom! And they weren't covered in cum. The aliens must have cleaned them after draining them of their fluids. And must have beamed them down to Remy's house. That was nice of them. Remy and Sam definitely needed some rest after becoming pussy milk machines. She wondered how much of their cum the lizards wound up taking with them. Did the grays keep any for themselves? Would Remy be juiced every time they abducted her from now on? And what other alien species would she be expected to fuck? She tingled at the thought of being dominated by more sexy extraterrestrials.

Sam stirred beside her. She yawned and opened her eyes. "Mmm, is it time for more alien fucking?"

Remy smiled and kissed her. "Nope. You're at my place."

"Huh?" Sam opened her eyes fully and looked around. "I'm in your room?"

"Yup."

"In your bed?"

"Yup."

"Woohoo! We had our first sleepover."

Remy laughed. "But we didn't get to watch cheesy sci-fi movies and eat junk food."

"We ate a lot of alien cum."

Remy giggled some more. "That's true. I guess that's almost as good as junk food." Alien cum was pretty tasty, but Remy had a serious sweet tooth. If she could eat junk food while getting fucked by aliens, that would be the best of both worlds.

Sam traced her fingers along Remy's bare body. "So the

aliens transported us to your place?"

"They must have. I don't remember anything after blacking out while they milked me."

"Me either. I didn't know I could cum that much."

Remy nodded. "I wonder what they're going to do with it."

"They're going to guzzle it down like a tasty milkshake!"

"More like a cum shake," Remy replied.

Sam tickled her. "I'll drink your cum shake anytime, Miss Sexy Assistant."

Remy smiled. "Good. I won't even charge you for it."

"You didn't charge the aliens either."

Remy tapped her lips. "Oh, that's true. But as the official Sex Ambassador for Earth, I can't be charging aliens for my cum. I must give it freely!" She thrust her hand out like she was performing the most noble duty on the planet.

Sam laughed. "You're so goofy."

"Me? You're the one creating sex robots."

"Well, that's just practical. How else do I turn nymphy co-eds into big sluts?"

"Wait, your whole goal has been to turn me into a slut?"

"Noooo. My goal is to turn all women into sluts. It's just a bonus I found such a sweet and beautiful slut like you."

"Oh, okay!" Remy liked Sam's compliment but still wasn't sure her new lover wasn't a mad sex scientist bent on taking over the world with an army of sluts. But that really didn't sound that bad, and Remy liked Sam too much to really worry about it. Plus, she was exhausted from being milked of all her juices, so she could worry about potential slutty world domination plans later.

"Did the aliens keep our clothes?" Sam asked.

"Dammit, they did it again!" Remy complained. "It happens every time I go up there."

"Maybe they're keeping them as artifacts."

"That would make sense except they usually disintegrate my clothes because they think I should always be naked."

Sam smirked. "They're smart aliens."

Remy launched her own tickle attack on her mischievous friend.

"In fact," Sam said, giggling. "I'm instituting a new policy. All sexy assistants must be nude in my lab."

"So I have to take my clothes off whenever I come work for you?"

"Yup."

"Okay, that sounds fair." Remy wasn't going to complain about being naked around Sam. She always wanted to strip whenever she was in the beautiful scientist's presence. Plus, T-69 would just rip her clothes off if she didn't remove them herself. He was like the aliens in not wanting her naughty parts covered. It was flattering so many people and creatures wanted Remy to constantly be naked.

Sam shifted her cute body against Remy's. "I really like

your bed."

"Wanna cuddle in it the rest of the day?" Remy asked hopefully.

"Heck yeah!"

They kissed and intertwined their limbs.

Remy sighed, feeling completely content and safe in Sam's arms.

That feeling didn't last long.

Her bedroom door burst open, a lone figure standing in the frame.

Remy gasped. "Mom!?!"

Remy and the Sex Monsters is a Kindle Vella Series with New Episodes Released Weekly! This book contains Episodes 16-31. Check out new sexy adventures beyond the events of this book at the Remy and the Sex Monsters Kindle Vella page or on your Android or iPhone.

Fully Nude and Erotic Covers are available on my Patreon page. You can get Nude and Sex Covers of this and other books as well as over one hundred naked/erotic pictures of my characters. Visit Patreon.com/RileyRoseErotica to check them out!

More Fun and Sexy Books

Little Red Riding Slut
Little Red Riding Slut is the biggest slut in all the land. Fortunately, she uses her sluttiness to defeat evildoers, so everyone loves her. Follow her adventures as she faces off against the Headless Horseman, anal-obsessed goblins, and a sexy witch who loves dominating naked sluts! Will Red be able to save the day with her epic sluttiness? Find out in this fun and sexy take on a classic fairytale!

Submitting to My Supernatural Neighbors
Elena Cortez lives in the best neighborhood ever, filled with all manner of sexy supernatural women. Though she has no idea about the paranormal powers of her soon-to-be paramours. Or how they'll make her the biggest supernatural slut in history! Will Elena give in to beautiful witch Cassia, curvy vampire Juliana, or muscular werewolf Kaia? Or all three at once? Find out if Elena can survive the ultimate tests of supernatural submission to her sexy and

powerful lovers!

Sex with My Robot Car

Mara Keoni is a sexy Navajo special agent who just got the unlikeliest of partners: the most advanced and kinky AI on the planet! Mara is teamed up with KATT, a female AI inside a super-up sports car. Who is not only eager to help Mara on her missions, but also eager to pleasure Mara in every way possible. Will Mara and KATT be able to stop the world's sexiest thief, Carla Santiago, and her band of beautiful criminals from committing the crime of the century?

Sexy Tentacles

Kione Ali is an adventurous treasure hunter, always looking to find the next big score. When she gets a clue to Blackbeard's treasure in Barbados, she can't pass up the opportunity to score the notorious pirate's booty. But she never expected to find a tentacle creature with the treasure, one that wants to pleasure Kione in every way possible and tie her up like the submissive sex object she is. Will Kione give in to her kinky curiosity to have tentacle sex? Will she let it explore every inch of her caverns? Find out in this sexy, sensual, tentacle adventure!

Visit RileyRoseErotica.com to get a Free eBook and check out more of my sexy books!

E-mail: Riley@RileyRoseErotica.com

Facebook: RileyRoseErotica
Twitter: @RileyRoserotica
Instagram: @RileyRoseErotica

About the Author

Riley Rose writes comedic, sexy stories featuring fun-loving female protagonists who love taking their clothes off. Discover sexy sci-fi, fantasy, and action/adventure worlds in over forty books and Kindle Vella stories, featuring naughty witches, frisky fairy tale characters, sex-obsessed robots, and titillating tentacles. You'll find fun, friendship, and a ton of submissive sex in Riley's books. Join the sexy shenanigans! Find out more at RileyRoseErotica.com.

Printed in Great Britain
by Amazon